Mural

Model Student Book One

Welcome to Model Student!

MURAL IS THE beginning of the *Model Student Series* by Devon Layne. The series comprises six books and is now available for order or pre-order. All beautifully designed and reasonably priced, Elder Road Books can be displayed with pride.

And for those who look inside, the characters and storyline will captivate as much as Devon's sensitive and sensuous sex scenes. Here's what readers have said:

A multi-part longer story, the characters feel like real people even though they are in a pretty rare type of arrangement.
They each struggle and fail and try again.
Great long read with fantastic sex scenes throughout.

An engaging and well-written story. But some of the writing, when describing Tony producing his masterpieces, is absolutely sublime.

It includes one of the most incredible sex scenes I've ever read.
Not the typical "insert tab A into slot B" nor
the bizarre "masturbatory fantasy played out with wooden models".

To order additional copies, see
https://www.createspace.com/6504352.
For more information and dealer pricing, contact
ElderRoadBooks@outlook.com or visit DevonLayne.com.

First paperback edition
ISBN 978-1-939275-44-8

Devon Layne

Mural

Model Student Book One

ELDER ROAD BOOKS
BELLEVUE, WA

ONE

IT WAS ONLY October and college was a bust. My best friend from high school was excited and having a great time—on the other coast. For me, it was depressing. I wasn't going to last until Thanksgiving.

It was my own fault, I suppose. I could have gone to the University of Nebraska and been an art major. Instead, I was blown away when The Pacific College of the Arts and Design, a small and exclusive college on the West Coast that was my 'reach' school, accepted me and I decided to attend. Not only that, but they'd offered me a financial aid package that meant I might escape college only about 30 grand in debt instead of 60. My portfolio was weak, but I'd managed to sell it well enough that the school actively recruited me and I fell for it. Now I was regretting it.

It wasn't very intellectually challenging. The school didn't offer a liberal arts BA; I was in a Bachelor of Fine Arts program. I had enjoyed the academic classes in high school and did well in both AP English and AP Math. But my only pseudo-liberal arts course in college was Art History taught by a boring old fossil. It was a three-hour class that met twice a week. We walked into class, he turned off the lights, turned on a slide projector, and everyone went to sleep.

The Fundamentals class was no better. We were 'taught' all the menial tasks of studio art. That meant six hours a week of stretching canvases, doing paint-overs, and scrubbing the studio floors. Over and over. Freshmen were pretty much the slaves of everyone else in the department. As far as I could tell there wasn't even a sophomore who cleaned his own brushes. How I managed to get both Studio Fundamentals and Visual Concepts the same year is beyond me. I guess it's because I got a pass from taking English Comp because of my high school AP scores, so they moved Concepts up a year.

The one bright spot in my schedule was my three-hour elective lab on Fridays in Figure Drawing. It combined basic anatomy drawing and live model drawing. There was a lot of sketching skeletons in the first three weeks, but then we had our first live model. Don't get excited. It was the professor's mother who came in and sat for a portrait sketch. In other words, she sat in a rocking chair and knitted for three hours while we drew her face and hands. The good part was that she had a really interesting face and you could tell she'd done this before because she really did hold a single expression for each of the posing sessions. Of course, she had the same expression on her face during her breaks.

Three weeks into school I had my golden birthday. That's when your age matches the day you're born on. I was 19 on September 19th. I had a phone call that night with my folks and about a dozen text messages with my best friend, Beth, out East. Nobody else knew—or cared. Whoopee.

Classes continued to drag on. I built frames, sized canvases, sorted fabric, wood, and metal scraps into bins, helped unload a massive rock from a truck, and burned my elbow on the kiln. Everything was crappy, including the weather. It was dark when I went to my first class and dark when I got back to my dorm room. I hardly ever heard from Beth anymore. Too busy. I called my folks every week, but they kept asking how it was going and I didn't want to tell them.

The high point of my week was going to a local racquet club to play racquetball. Dad had insisted that I have some physical exercise while I was at college. I was going to an art school. There wasn't even a gym. Racquetball was the best I could do, and I liked playing. Still, that was only a few hours a week and I was tempted to quit that, too, if it wasn't for the one hottie that I sometimes got to play against. She was some kind of national champion, so she creamed me on a regular basis, but just watching her work up a sweat was usually good for keeping my spirits and other things up another couple of hours—or until I got back to the dorm.

It wasn't until late October that we got our first nude model in Figure Drawing. We knew something was up when we came into the studio that Friday and the temperature was about ten degrees higher than normal. Professor McIntyre explained that this was for the comfort of the model. I was sweating. The model was a woman about forty years old, who I recognized from sketches that decorated the walls from years past. She was a little overweight, but I guess attractive enough. Not enough to be beating off to her image that night. I looked around the studio briefly when she had taken her first pose. None of the other students seemed all that enthused about drawing her either.

Of course, all the other students in the class were girls. Five of the twenty of us were freshmen. This model certainly wasn't showing any of them anything they weren't already intimately familiar with. We drew and I actually left with a couple pretty decent sketches. There were nineteen other women in the class I'd rather have been looking at naked.

On the way out of class, three of my favorites who I had lunch with on many Fridays fell into step on either side of me. I could tell something was up.

"Well, did you get an eyeful?" Sandra asked.

"That wasn't your first time seeing a naked woman, was it?" Melody joined in.

"Didn't she just get you all hot?"

"Did you sprout a woody? You stayed behind your easel the whole class," Amy asked.

"Oh come on, you guys. She's a model. Who's going to get turned on while they're drawing?"

"Don't tell me you aren't interested in women!" Melody sounded shocked.

"All right," Sandra rejoined, "we'll have to hold this conversation after we've had a male model. It's no fun teasing someone who won't get embarrassed." Actually, at that mention I *was* embarrassed. I was—shall we say—sexually inexperienced, but I wasn't gay. All my life, though, people just assumed that if you were a male artist, you must be gay. Granted, I was sensitive, quiet, and a bit shy around girls, but I was definitely interested in them. Melody, especially. She was about 5'2" and nicely shaped. I'd done a few covert sketches of her when I was supposed to be drawing hands or feet of a model. Back in my room, I'd even enhanced a few of them into imagined nudes. I thought about the shape of her breasts and the size of her nipples. It wasn't like I hadn't noticed when they hardened under her t-shirt. Women don't seem to have any more control over the headlights than guys have over their cocks.

Mural

Talking to her was something altogether different. I was fine as long as we were just palling around the cafeteria or the studio, but I'd never be able to ask her out. The few times I'd been with her without another friend, I hadn't been able to say two words. Besides, I'd heard she had a big scary boyfriend. I was relieved that Sandra and Amy were always around. The three amigas. I don't think I could have been alone with Melody and survived.

It took me all of two weeks at school to figure out why I'd been recruited so aggressively by the admissions office. I was the only guy in studio arts who wanted to study painting instead of animation. At first I'd just thought it was weird that I had a Figure Drawing class with nineteen girls and me. It's the same as when I was in high school. Guy in art? Of course, he must be gay, right?

I DIDN'T GO home over Thanksgiving break. It's over 1,500 miles and we aren't rich. I ate turkey loaf in the cafeteria. We still hadn't seen a male nude in Figure Drawing. It wasn't like we had a lot of body builders in the art school lining up to model. In high school it was like a big initiation for the jocks to model for the senior art class after they turned eighteen. Pay was never mentioned. School rules said the guys had to wear jockstraps. Girls had to wear bikinis.

The first Friday of December, we were finally expecting this older guy, who'd done one of our portrait sessions, to show up as our first male nude.

Dr. Bychkova, my art history professor stopped me in the hall before class to ask about my progress on some stupid paper I was supposed to write, so I was late walking into the studio.

The semicircle of easels had been pulled a little closer around the posing platform and every single one of my nineteen classmates was in position waiting. Don't ever believe that women aren't as curious about the opposite sex as men. They'd been waiting for this day all semester. Even Amy had managed a spot near the center, and she's definitely gay. I got the last position at the end of the semicircle where, if I was lucky, I'd see a profile of the model's head and one butt cheek. It would be a great drawing. Ha ha. Professor McIntyre came into the class and walked to the dais. She gave a sigh.

"I'm sorry," she said. "Mr. Johnson (yeah that was his real name) called in sick. I just got the word from the office. Since we don't have a model, we'll work from a manikin for today."

"No fair!" The girl who blurted out the sentiments of all the girls in the class was Sandra, and her easel was dead center. She'd probably come in twenty minutes early to get that spot. But she wasn't the only one grumbling. There was a general dissent in the class.

"What can I do?" Prof asked. "I can't materialize a model out of thin air. Believe me, this class would be a lot easier to teach if I could."

"Let Tony model." I almost swallowed the pencil I had between my teeth as I was fastening paper to my easel. *Me? Who made that suggestion?* I looked across the easels and saw Melody grinning broadly.

"That suggestion is flawed. Tony hasn't asked or agreed to model. If he had, it is still inappropriate to expose a classmate. I'd say the same thing if you had suggested a woman. And it would be unfair to Tony to spend three hours posing and not drawing."

"I don't mind." *Was that my voice that just spoke?* Geez! What was I doing? Professor McIntyre looked at me. I felt the heat rise in my face and knew I was red. But, shit! *Melody* had just asked to see me naked. "Um… I mean… I'd rather not draw pictures of a manikin, anyway. I assume that by 'being exposed,' you mean my privates and I've got a jockstrap in my bag. I could wear that." I was getting redder the longer I talked. I'd just told a class full of girls that I was carrying a jockstrap!

"You just happen to have an athletic supporter in your bag when you attend this class, Tony?"

"I usually go play racquetball after class on Fridays. It's my gym bag."

"And do you have your racquet with you as well?"

"Yes, ma'am." There was total silence in the room as Professor McIntyre thought about it. You could feel the tension from the girls.

"Are there any students here who would feel uncomfortable having Tony model for the class while wearing an athletic sup-porter? Anyone at all in any way? Please be absolutely free to speak up. If it would make you embarrassed to have your class-mate up here, say so. This is an art class. Art is not necessarily sexuality. The purpose of this class is to study the figure, not to embarrass or titillate. Please say now if this proposition is not okay with you." I almost raised my hand, but I'd committed. I wasn't going to back down now. No one in the class said a word. If I had to guess, I'd say they were all holding their breath.

"Okay. Tony, if you are sure you are okay with this, then please step behind the drape and get ready. Bring your racquet out with you. I'd like to see some action poses."

Action poses. Right.

While I stripped off behind the drape and put on my jock I could hear Professor McIntyre continue to lecture the girls in the class quietly. She made it very clear that if they could not maintain a professional attitude when "the model" was on stage that class would be immediately dismissed.

I'd worked with nude models before. We had a pretty progressive art program in high school and students who were over eighteen years old were invited to a weekly sitting that was technically not on school grounds, but still had 'club' status. It was held at the local art store where several art classes were held. The owner brought a model in from Omaha once a week. None of us knew who he or she was and we seldom saw the same person twice. But I knew what needed to be done.

When Prof asked if I was ready, I took a deep breath and croaked out the word "yes." I walked out onto the dais and kept my eyes focused on Prof, intentionally not looking at anyone else in the class.

"Tony, I presume this is your first time as a model. Keep in mind that you need to make sure you are comfortable in your pose and can hold it for fifteen minutes. We'll change poses then, and again at half an hour. At forty-five minutes, you get a fifteen-minute break. Don't do anything that forces you to hold a strenuous pose. No balancing on your toes or one leg or anything. Let's start with a common racquetball pose. You're waiting for the serve. Feet shoulder width apart, knees slightly bent, racquet in front held in both hands, facing straight forward." I had no idea that Prof knew so much about racquetball.

I'm not particularly self-conscious about my body—most of it. It's not like I'm ripped or anything, but at nineteen, I'm not overweight either. Sometimes I even manage to play racquetball *twice* in a week if I can escape from homework. So I guess I was in pretty good shape. Posing like I was waiting for the serve was an easy thing to do. The model platform was raised about a foot-and-a-half above the floor so artists could look over their drawing pads and see the model. That meant that if I looked straight ahead, I was looking over the tops of my classmates and didn't have to make eye contact with any of them. I reminded myself that they were just a roomful of artists and not nineteen sexy female classmates.

I just stood there in the pose Prof had dictated. In my mind's eye I built the end wall of the court and could almost see where the ball would hit. When her timer went off at fifteen minutes, I found myself in a Zen-like trance. I don't know where I went while my body posed, but as soon as Prof directed me into a backhand position, I returned there. I held my racquet in my hand in one position and could imagine what it would look like on paper. I could see the strings in their weave and the tension in my own muscles. I knew that if I left the class right now, I could draw the same pose. The class flew by. Before I knew it, Prof told me to go back and get dressed. When I came out five minutes later, the girls all applauded and said thank you. All told, it was pretty cool.

With racquetball after lunch and getting to play against Lissa, the cute champion, I didn't get depressed again until I woke up Saturday morning.

TWO

I **PACKED** my whole dorm room up with neatly labeled boxes to ship home. I hadn't told my folks yet that I wasn't coming back to PCAD. I hated it.

If anything, Christmas break was even more depressing than my first semester had been. My best friend didn't come home. Apparently her parents had arranged to have Christmas in Hawaii and she flew straight back to the East Coast. I hung out with a couple of guys from high school, but all I could see was how much we had become different. I guess that's one thing about high school; no matter how individual you are, you all share twelve years of common experiences. Suddenly, you've all gone to college or to jobs and your paths diverge. I was a little envious of them because they all talked like they loved what they were doing.

Dad and I played racquetball at the YMCA a couple times. That had always been something we did as father and son. I really enjoyed it and Dad told me he thought I was really improving. I guess I did mention that Lissa kept me sharp so I wouldn't embarrass myself.

The UPS truck brought my boxes the day after Christmas. Great. I was having a Boxing Day. Mom asked me about them, but I just said that I didn't need this stuff at school. I don't know why I kept avoiding telling them I wasn't going back. I spent my time in my room writing personal essays for my transfer application to UNeb. It sucked that they don't let anyone know until June or July. By that time, I could be in the Navy. Navy sounded like a safe bet since there wasn't any water around Omaha.

I wandered, too. It was cold and there was a foot of snow on the fields. I trudged out to some of my favorite places to draw and did my best to capture the cold, desolate feeling while keeping my gloves on and mopping my constantly running nose on my sleeve. I realized my eyes were running a lot, too, but I blamed that on the cold wind.

I was supposed to be at PCAD to become an artist. I unpacked my drawings from first semester to show my appreciative parents, but as I looked at them I saw what was happening to me. The technique was good. I was learning a lot about how to control shading and contour. In fact, compared to my earlier drawings and paintings, they were far superior. But they lacked any sense of emotion. When I looked at them I thought a computer could have drawn it just as well.

Winter break was showing me something else. I didn't want to live at home. I'd missed my parents so much while I was in Seattle, but now that we were together all day every day, I was going stir crazy. I'd never make it till spring if I stayed here. Two days before my flight was scheduled to return me to Seattle, I packed up my boxes and took them to the UPS office. I didn't ship as many back as I'd brought in the fall. I needed clothes, art supplies, and my racquetball equipment. Two boxes, plus the suitcase I'd carry on with me. Yeah. I'd decided that even another semester at Hell U would be better than staying holed up in Nebraska for the rest of the winter.

―――⊲◆⊳―――

GRADES CAME OUT and I hadn't done badly, even in the class I thought I was failing. After the break, I thought I was ready for another term. "Never make a life-changing decision before you go on vacation," my dad had said when I was trying to choose a college in the first place. It seemed like good advice and I was almost looking forward to the challenges of the next semester.

It took almost two weeks before I was thinking about quitting and heading back to Nebraska again. I didn't *fit* in this city. It was constantly gray and drizzling rain. I couldn't imagine ever being warm and dry again. Even though Nebraska was colder, it was bright and sunny and there would be a fire in the fireplace at night.

I had no friends to speak of. I didn't want to spend my time hanging out with the stoners in the dorm, so I was spending most of my time alone. Or in the gym. I saw a lot of my classmates with their noses up against their iPhones or playing on some game machine. I wanted to beat on something and a racquetball was pretty safe. Most of the time it didn't beat back.

Sure there were people I saw every day. There were even a few that I had lunch with regularly. Melody, Sandra, and Amy seemed to catch up with me in the cafeteria more frequently than just our Friday class together. I didn't really hang out with anyone, though. Back in high school, at least there were a few people I considered close friends. Here at art school, we were all outcaste. Even from each other. I never saw anyone smile.

The second semester studio class was Figure Painting. The old guy, Mr. Johnson, came in twice to model. Maybe it gave the girls a thrill to stare at a real live cock dangling in front of a guy. God, he was hung. I fervently hoped the girls didn't think that was how guys were supposed to look. They'd be really disappointed someday. I played racquetball at least three times a week now and just battered the hell out of the ball in the one session I where I practiced alone.

We were told the last half of our Figure Painting class would be spent primarily working on a final project. When we got the assignment, our lunch table was buzzing with brainstorms.

"I know what you're doing," Melody taunted me. "Something with drapes. Probably watercolor."

"Don't forget the nude and the dog," I said. "It *is* Figure Painting. But, yeah. There will be drapes."

"I'm going to develop that sketch I did of the hippie chick model in highlights against a dark background," Sandra said.

"She was cool," said Amy. "I might do one of her. In fact, I'd love to do her." She got a dreamy look on her face and we all stared at her. Yeah, lesbians get lovesick, too. She realized we were all staring. "I just don't know what positi… which pose to do. What about you, Melody?"

"Uh… I was thinking something classical. Like maybe an oil of *The Discus Thrower* or something."

"Who's going to model?"

"I'll probably just go to the museum and find a sculpture," Melody sighed. I was sure she had blushed. Well, old man Johnson was sure no model for that kind of painting. Maybe *The Dick Thrower*. We all had different places to be after lunch and I grabbed my gym bag to go play racquetball. I was suddenly aware that Melody hadn't gone with the others. She was still standing beside me.

"Is it hard to play racquetball?" she asked.

"Um… Not really—at least not the basics." *Why was it so hard to talk to her without everyone else around?* "If you get to competitive levels, there's as many nuances as there are in tennis. Anybody can play, but there are really only a few that reach Wimbledon."

"Do you compete?"

"Every match is a competition. When you play at a gym, sometimes you are playing with guys—or gals—who are a lot better than you are. Sometimes, you're the better one. You learn from masters and teach novices. To answer your question fairly, I was in a few YMCA tournaments back in high school, but haven't done anything but gym tournaments and individual matches since I got here. I do it for fun."

"Would you mind if I watched sometime?"

"No. Just let me know and I'll get you a club pass."

"Today?" I jerked around to look at her. Like always, her auburn hair and strikingly lavender eyes just took my breath away. Had she really just invited herself along with me to the gym?

"Sure. If you want to."

"Great! Tell me what the basic rules are while we walk over so I can understand what's going on."

I told her all about the game rules. Racquetball uses all six surfaces of an enclosed room. That meant people who watched the game only saw the match through the back glass wall. I also told her that if she got bored she was free to go—she didn't have to wait for me. I went to change and showed up at the court at my appointed time.

I'd forgotten that my opponent today was Lissa, a nice lady and a fierce competitor. Okay. Not just a nice lady. A gorgeous lady. An object-of-my-fantasies lady. A sooo-far-out-of-my-league lady. What a day to have Melody watching. I was going to get my ass handed to me on a silver platter. I was a little self-conscious about having someone I knew watching me—especially someone as cute and nice as Melody—but when Lissa's first serve went sailing past me, I got focused fast. It didn't take long before I was fighting for my life on the court and forgot all about my spectator.

———————⊲◆⊳———————

"WOW! THAT WAS something else," Melody said as we exited through the low door from the court.

"Oh! You're still here."

"Who's your friend, Tony?"

"Lissa, this is my classmate Melody. Melody, this is Lissa. She's a champion."

"That was really amazing. Tony didn't mention that he was playing a woman. A really beautiful woman."

"Thank you. It's nice to meet you, too, Melody. Tony, you're showering here, aren't you?"

"Yeah. I like to get a steam and a hot tub after a match. You?"

"Yes. I thought maybe your date would like a steam and soak, too. It's better than waiting out here alone for you."

"We're not…" I began.

"Thanks but I didn't bring a towel or anything," Melody jumped in.

"No problem," Lissa said. "We'll get you a guest pass. Everything you need is in the locker room." It was pretty clear that Lissa wasn't taking no for an answer and as I headed for the showers, Lissa and Melody headed for the ladies' locker room. That made showering a little embarrassing. Every time I thought about the two of them lounging around the women's steam room or spa, I started to get hard. Getting hard is not something I wanted to do in the men's locker room. I sought shelter in the dense steam until I regained control of myself, then took a cold shower, and rushed to my locker to get dressed.

I needn't have hurried. I was the one waiting outside the locker room when Melody and Lissa finally exited. They were laughing like old friends and Lissa gave Melody a hug before she left. I stood there staring at Melody. She was wearing the same clothes she had at school, but apparently Lissa had helped apply a little makeup after their shower. The woman I was looking at was heart-stoppingly beautiful.

"She is so cool!" Melody laughed. "She told me all about competing and her home and her two kids. Did you know she's a model? I mean a professional model!"

"Wait. Lissa has kids?"

"Don't you know anything? Yeah. Damon is six and Drew is four. She sure is in great shape for a mom, don't you think?"

"No kidding."

"You know what else? I asked her if she'd model for our class."

"No way!"

"She said yes! I'm going to give her number to Professor McIntyre."

"I'll die in that class. Lissa? Really?" I said. I was feeling cramped in my pants already.

"Let's get dinner at Dixie's," Melody said. I looked my question at her. She had the good grace to blush. "Sorry. I suppose you've got a date. Never mind."

"No! I mean… It's Friday night. Don't *you* have a date?"

"Duh! If I had a date, I wouldn't have asked you out."

"You asked me out?"

"What? I need to be more formal? Tony, would you go out to dinner with me tonight? I know this nice barbecue joint called Dixie's. It's nothing fancy, but if you're not busy I'd love to go out with you. There. Is that better?" Melody was turning bright pink, and so was I.

"No. I mean, no, you didn't have to be formal. Yes, I'd love to go to dinner with you. It just surprised me. I didn't… Wow! I thought you had a serious boyfriend."

"Vicious rumor. Besides, I just want to talk to you… you know… about our final project." Oh. So that was it. It wasn't really a *going out* type date. It was kind of a *study date*. Oh well. I could live with that. I just needed to keep the images of Melody and Lissa in the hot tub out of my head.

We didn't bother going back to our dorms first. We just changed directions and walked the six blocks over to Dixie's. We were early enough that it wasn't too crowded yet and we split a full rack of ribs that was to die for. I was so caught off guard that I didn't have time to worry about whether I could talk to Melody. It just happened. We had barbecue sauce up to our elbows and were laughing so much that I didn't realize until we were leaving that we hadn't talked about the final project at all.

"Uh, did you want to talk about the final project?" I asked when we were still a couple blocks from the dorms.

"Oh yeah. I almost forgot." Melody was quiet for a long time and I decided that maybe the project was just an excuse to go have a good time together after all. When she finally spoke it was in a rush and it almost blew me away. "Would you be my model? I want to develop one of the sketches of you playing racquetball into my final project and I'd like you to pose for me."

"You mean…?" I made a vague gesture at my clothes.

"Yeah. Nude," she said. She was definitely blushing now. "Oh god. This is so dumb. We never had male models in my high school art program. Mr. Johnson is the only naked male I've ever seen. This is so difficult. It's just to pose."

"Yeah, well, I mean… You might not like what you see any better." Like I said, I'm not particularly self-conscious about my body… except for one thing. I'm hung like a hamster. Everything is functional, and according to the books I've read, I'm completely average when I'm erect. But when I'm just carrying it around, it shrivels up like a prune. The whole time I was posing for the class last semester, I scarcely created a bulge in my jock. And there was no way that Melody wouldn't be comparing me to Johnson's johnson. "I'd like to, but…"

"I'll trade," she squeaked. "I'll model for you with all your drapery hanging around if you'll model for me."

"Sure… um… Wow! That's… really fair. Um… I don't think Professor McIntyre will let us do that in the studio, though," I said. Who was I kidding? If Melody Anderson was willing to get naked for me, I'd rent a room somewhere if I needed to. "We'll just have to find our own makeshift studio. You'd really do it?"

"I've had it in mind ever since the day you posed for the class. I hope you don't think I'm stalking or something. It's just for the art… uh… you know."

"Yeah. Just for the art."

THREE

I LEFT THE PLANNING to Melody. She said she had an idea and would let me know when we could work. In the meantime, true to her word, Lissa showed up in our studio the first Friday morning in February.

Sweet Jesus! I had never seen anything so incredible in my life. The woman who regularly beat me to a pulp playing racquetball at least once a week was there in front of me stark naked and looking like a goddess come to life. Lissa is about five-ten, the same as me. She's a real athlete with an amazing rack that just plain doesn't move, even without her sports bra. She's blonde up top and there was no way to tell about below because she was shaved smooth. When she was introduced, Prof said something about a real atelier model in our midst.

I didn't quite have a six pack, but Lissa did. Not the gross bodybuilder kind, but the kind that was so flat and firm that you could see her muscles ripple beneath her skin. I knew from playing racquetball that she was graceful, but as a nude model in front of our class, she was like a panther stalking and then freezing with her muscles quivering, ready to pounce.

Yeah, I acted all professional and everything, but as soon as class was over and she stepped behind the curtain, I looked at what I'd drawn and sprouted an instant boner. When I looked at some of the girls, they looked a little glassy-eyed, too. After class, Lissa stopped to talk to Melody and when I caught up she turned and smiled at me.

"We're still on for this afternoon, right?" she asked.

"Huh?" *Oh my god! We're going to play racquetball this afternoon.* "Yeah. See you later."

———◁◆▷———

"SEE YOU LATER? Don't tell me you have a date with that… that… that goddess!" Amy squealed as we walked into the cafeteria.

"We play racquetball every week," I said meekly.

"Yeah, sure. She bats your balls around, I'll bet," Sandra smirked.

"Really."

"Yeah, really. I'll be there to chaperone," Melody said. I looked at her with my mouth open. She was coming to watch us play again? Since the last time she came to the club and we went out to dinner, we hadn't managed to get together once. What can I say? Stupid school. As boring as most of my classes were, it was still a ton of work. Fundamentals class had advanced from hours of stretching canvases to hours of prepping a huge mural wall that the instructor was doing for the school. It was listed as lab, but it was just grunt work.

I bet that when Michelangelo painted the Sistine Chapel, it was probably him and about thirty freshman students who mixed paint, plaster, and ran errands for him. If he was working, they were working. That's how the fundamentals professor was. We'd spent most of the past four weekends working or on call for hours to do the grunt work. It's the only other class I have with Melody, but I didn't see her once when I was working.

Melody and I got to the club and she had a guest pass wait-ing for her. She headed straight for the ladies' locker room. I went to change and headed for the court. When I got there, Lissa was already showing Melody the proper stance for receiv-ing a serve. She had her arms wrapped around Melody's waist to reach her hands on the racquet. It was sexy as hell.

"Tony, serve a couple of lobs for Melody. Don't go crazy. I promised I'd show her the fundamentals of play today and then we'll have our game."

"I don't mind," I answered truthfully. Melody was dressed in a tank top over a sports bra and a pair of short shorts that showed the lower crease of her butt. And every time I looked at Lissa, I still saw her naked in my mind's eye with her per-fect breasts and bullet-like nipples and her smoothly shaved pussy. Of course, they were both behind me when I served, but I quickly backpedaled to give Melody and Lissa room to return the ball. I was still watching the two follow through when the ball hit me in the chest. Melody screeched and asked if I was all right. Lissa just rolled her eyes at me and threw me the ball to serve again.

We worked like that for about fifteen or twenty minutes and then Lissa said it was time for her to get my attention back on the ball, so a very winded Melody left the court to watch as Lissa worked my ass off chasing her serves from one side of the court to the other. I was amazed that I actually managed to score a few points; she really took me to school.

"Mercy!" I finally yelled, falling on my knees after the last point. "I'm no match for you today."

"You are *never* a match for me," Lissa laughed. "That's for having your head in a different room this afternoon. Seriously,

Tony, you're the only real competition I have here so I need you to have your head in the game." She gave me one of the most evil looks I have ever seen as we turned to the low door. "Now I'm going to take your girlfriend to the showers and get naked with her," she whispered in my ear. "Think about that for a while."

"She's not my…"

"Yeah. Sure."

Melody and Lissa left me standing outside the racquetball court, already getting hard.

———◁◆▷———

"Next weekend," Melody said out of the blue as we were eating that night. I'd done my best imitation of her formal invite and she'd accompanied me to The Twister, a retro café with a lot of 60s paraphernalia hanging on the walls. I looked at her blankly, not comprehending the *non sequitur*.

"Next weekend is when we work on our final project. We'll have all weekend, so plan to skip racquetball that Friday and not get back until Sunday night. Pack your sketch supplies and paints and the canvas or watercolor paper you intend to use. I've made arrangements to borrow two easels from the studio so we won't have to dismantle one piece in order to work on the other. Don't bother packing much in the way of clothes. I expect we'll be naked most of the weekend."

I blew Coke out my nose.

"Where are we going?"

"I've got it all arranged. I've even got a car for the weekend to transport our stuff. Don't worry about it. Just be ready to go after class."

———◁◆▷———

IT WAS A *damn* fine day. Lissa even called to tell me she was out of town and had to cancel our court time.

True to her word, Melody dragged me away from class without so much as stopping for lunch with our friends. We lugged two easels downstairs to where a Mazda SUV was sitting and loaded them in the back. Then Melody drove us to the dorms to load anything else we needed and in twenty minutes we were on the road. It wasn't a long drive. We drove up Queen Anne, weaving around dead ends where the street couldn't make the grade and finally winding around to the west side of the hill. I assumed we must be headed to Melody's home, as confidently as she was driving, but the place we stopped at was nothing less than stunning. The house was in a nice neighborhood and looked elegant from the front, but when she led me through to the back of the house, I was speechless. From the back deck there was an absolutely spectacular view of the water. The early afternoon sun was sparkling off the surface.

"This place is beautiful!" I said. "Is this where you live?"

"No. I borrowed it for the weekend. We'll be working downstairs. Let's get our stuff." We unloaded the car and this time Melody led me down the front stairs into a walkout basement. The view was almost as good here as it was from upstairs, but only from the sliding glass doors. The rest of the room had been cleared of everything but the essentials. At one end of the room was a twin sleigh bed stacked with linens, pillows, and fabric. At the other end of the room, easily thirty feet long, was a hardwood floor. It looked like a dance floor… or a racquetball court. The ceiling was nowhere near high enough, but it didn't take much imagination to see it as a sports court setting. I was pretty sure Melody wasn't planning to draw the ceiling.

"This is so cool! We can set your scene up at this end and mine at that end."

"You figured it out. I was afraid I was going to have to explain."

"I may be slow, but I'm not stopped. I don't know how you managed to arrange this but you are brilliant. But there's like… um… one thing… You might not like everything you see and… um…"

"Look, just set up your scene and I'll set up mine. We can flip a coin to see who goes first." With that she started setting up her easel and sketchbook while I started working on the drapery the way I imagined it.

"This bed is perfect. How did you manage this?"

"That Watteau painting you said you liked when we were talking about drapery—*The Toilet*. And the picture you showed me by Boucher—*Resting Maiden*. This reminded me of those. I just figured you could alter the headboard and fabrics when you paint."

"You put a lot of thought into this, Melody. Thank you. This just happened to be here?"

"Pretty much."

I wasn't sure what that meant, but I was so excited about setting the scene that I didn't investigate any further. Behind the bed, there was an adjustable coat rack to hang the drapes over. I made up the bed with pillows and hung my tricot drapes. When I framed the image between my hands, the drapes looked like they were suspended from skyhooks. I had a few props that I'd brought with me, as well. I positioned the ewer and bowl that I found in the theater props closet on a small table at the end of the bed. I went up to the kitchen and washed the purple grapes that I'd bought that morning at the market and brought them down in a bowl. I positioned candles strategically around the scene. I knew exactly what I wanted and where. When I was finished, I turned toward Melody at the other end of the room. She didn't have much in the way of props, but she'd thought to bring two flood lights with diffusion screens with her to create a bright corner of the room without casting shadows.

Melody looked at my setup and nodded. I looked at hers and wandered around under the lights checking for shadows as well. We met back in the middle.

"Should we…?"

"You want a Coke?" We spoke at about the same time and laughed at our own nervousness.

"There's no rush," Melody said. "Why don't we go upstairs and have a little lunch before we get started? My stomach's growling." I'd been so focused on getting set up that I forgot about food, but as soon as she mentioned it I became acutely aware of my own hunger pangs.

"Great idea. Should we go get burgers?"

"Our… um… host left us food in the fridge."

"Is our host coming back while we're here?" I asked as I followed her up the stairs.

"Out of town. Oh. We have the bedroom on the left down the hall."

"We?"

"Um… or any of the others, I guess. That's just the one she pointed out to me." Melody pulled a platter of cold cuts and cheese out of the fridge with mustard and mayo. There was a loaf of bread and a knife on the counter. We made sandwiches and drank Cokes in silence.

"Tony."

"Melody." We started at the same time again. This time she nodded to me to go first.

"Melody, this place is cool and all, but are you comfortable here… I mean, alone with me? You know I'm not expecting anything but modeling, don't you?"

"I kinda suggested it, remember? And I should be asking you those questions. I mean, I understand if you really *don't* like girls, but Lissa said we all had that wrong. But, if you're not into *me*… I still want to do the painting with you, and I won't ask for anything else."

My heart was beating like a thousand times a second. Melody, my secret fantasy girl, was telling me she might be up for more if I was interested. When I stood up I wavered a second, afraid I was going to pass out from lack of oxygen. I went around the little breakfast bar and stood in front of Melody. She looked up at me with… I wanted to say hope, but I thought there was fear, too. I took her hands in mine.

"Melody, there isn't anything you could ask of me this weekend that I wouldn't give you. It's really more than okay." I pulled her up from her seat, thinking that we'd head back to the makeshift studio, but she melted against me and pressed her lips to mine. It was soft and gentle and lingered with tastes of hope and promise.

"Let's see how it goes," she whispered.

———◁◆▷———

THE NEXT ORDER of business was to determine who went first. Would I model and she paint or the other way around? Melody pulled out a coin from her bag and told me to call it in the air. She tossed the coin up and I yelled, "Heads!" The coin hit the floor and started rolling across the hardwood. We both chased after it, laughing. It rolled all the way into the corner and ended up leaning against the baseboard.

"Okay, I guess we know what that means," she said. I looked at her blankly. "We both go at the same time."

"We can't both paint and model at the same time."

"No, but we can both undress at the same time. That's what all the uncertainty is about, isn't it? I'm afraid you'll think I'm not beautiful like Lissa and you're afraid I won't like your cock as much as old man Johnson's. So, we both undress at the same time and we just stay that way this weekend. Ready, set, go. Please don't hesitate or I won't have the courage to keep going," she squealed as she peeled off her t-shirt and reached behind to unsnap her bra. I quickly pulled off my shirt as well and then we both kicked off our shoes and shimmied out of our jeans and underwear in one move. In less than fifteen seconds we were both naked.

Oh god, she was beautiful! My eyes started up from her toes and got stuck for a minute on her bare pussy. She'd shaved it like Lissa's. I don't know why I kept thinking about Lissa except that she'd been modeling for us last week and… I wrenched my eyes further up and saw two of the most exquisite breasts I'd ever imagined. I couldn't wait to touch… I mean paint them. When my eyes reached her face I discovered hers were still glued to my crotch, her mouth hanging open.

My tiny little cock. *Shit.*

"Tony?" I glanced down and realized that my cock was rapidly expanding from a one-inch flop to a six-inch monster as she watched.

"I… I'm sorry. It kind of does that when I… well… whenever I even think about you naked." At last her eyes rose to meet mine.

"You think about me naked?" I nodded. "That's so sweet!" She rushed at me and the kiss she planted on my lips this time extended all the way to the back of my throat. My cock was throbbing against her stomach as she pulled back away from me. The first time it had ever actually touched a girl. "Maybe we should wait until it's dark outside to start painting. So we can control the light better."

"What should we do till then?" I whispered, touching her lips again.

"We could go unpack our things in the bedroom and see if… the bed… is comfortable."

"We have a bed right here," I said, pointing to the draped setting I'd created at the end of the room. She kissed me again and I lifted her, carrying her to the bed I'd set for my painting.

"Tony," she whispered as I began trailing kisses down her neck and torso. "Oh, Tony. I've been hoping for this since we first met. I was so afraid that you didn't like girls, or that you just didn't like me."

"God, Melody. I'm so stupid. I just thought a girl like you… I mean someone who's so pretty… and smart… and talented… would never be interested in somebody like me. I should have said something, but I was just so busy hating school that I couldn't imagine you wanted anything more than a lunch partner." I reached her left nipple and kissed it, caressing it with my tongue. The whimper she made and the pressure of her hand on the back of my head told me I was doing something right. I'd studied all the basic mechanics of the human body as an art student, but I didn't really have any practical experience when it came to touching one. She pulled at me and lifted my head to return to her lips.

"I want you to explore all my body this weekend and I want to explore you, too, so don't think I don't *want* you to lick me. But what I really want first, is to feel you in me. Tony, before we do anything else, can we just make love?"

"Like I told you, Mel. We can do anything you want."

"Gently."

"Melody… I've never…"

"Me either. But I really want to. I want you."

I could feel her fingers wrapped around my penis as she stroked the head up and down her moist slit. The combined fluids quickly coated both of us. She positioned the head against her opening and began pulling me slowly into her. I was holding myself back, afraid I'd hurt her or lose control—not knowing what I was doing and not wanting it to ever end. When I was fully inside her she gasped and locked her lips on mine again. We kissed long and deep, not moving below the waist, but just feeling the magic of being joined together—realizing that in those few moments we'd made the transition and were no longer virgins.

For a moment, I was frozen. No wonder I hated school. It was why I'd never asked Melody out. I'd almost let this beautiful woman pass by. And now, she'd just reached into my heart and started it beating again. We pulled back from our kiss enough to look into each other's eyes and found that we were both crying. I hugged her, kissed her, wept with her, all the time just joined as deeply as we could get. I didn't care about having an orgasm. I didn't care that I was no longer a virgin. All I cared about was that I was so profoundly accepted by this incredible woman. Not just accepted. Loved.

When we finally began to move, sliding together and apart, we kept looking into each other's eyes and holding each other in awe. We were one. We were all there was in the world. When our orgasms came crashing over us, it was enough to knock us both out. I succeeded in getting an arm under myself so all my weight wouldn't crush her. With our cheeks pressed tightly against each other, I couldn't tell if I tasted her tears or my own.

———◁◆▷———

"WAIT," I WHISPERED. "Don't move." I'd somehow slid off her, out of her. She still lay sprawled back across the bed. Her left leg was pulled up and leaned close to her outstretched right leg. Her head was thrown back against the pillows and her left arm was raised over her head. Her right hand lay on her stomach, now that I no longer did.

I lit the candles, reached for my sketchbook, and began working furiously. It was perfect—the drapery, the light, the position of the ewer. Her breathing was music to me and I lost myself in the gentle rise and fall of her breasts. Her eyes as she looked at me—their violet depths captured my very soul. I placed a small bunch of grapes in her left hand, dangling above her head. She barely glanced at them. A perfect model. In fifteen minutes, I had captured a sketch that I could transfer to my watercolor board. I was completely in love.

"You know," she said softly, speaking for the first time since we'd made love. "You're going to have to do that every time you want me to pose this weekend."

I figured I could live with that.

FOUR

"**M**ELODY, TONY, could I see you please?" Prof. McIntyre led the two of us to a corner of the studio where we couldn't easily be overheard by the rest of the class. We were working with pastels today and the model was the 20-year-old hippie chick Amy liked so much. She was one of those totally *au naturel* women who didn't shave anything. You had to wonder if the hair that hung almost to the waist was from her head or her armpits. Yeah, I joke like that. Actually she was a very sweet looking woman with one of those willowy figures that makes you think of Galadriel or something. I wasn't happy being called away from my easel.

Prof had our drawings in front of her. We handed them in on Monday and figured we were way ahead of the rest of the class because that phase of the project wasn't due until today. We were almost finished with the whole project after our weekend. We really did do some work besides just falling into bed with each other every couple of hours.

"These are nice work from both of you," Prof began. I could just hear the "but" that hadn't yet been spoken. "Unfortunately, they won't be usable for your final project." Both of us gasped and looked at each other. "How far are you with these paintings?"

"Nearly finished," I answered.

"You're working ahead."

"Is that a problem?"

"In this instance, yes. This is a process project. I've no doubt that the pieces you are painting are excellent works of art. You both show incredible talent and as long as you both have model releases from each other, I can't prevent you from displaying them in the end term exhibition. But they won't do for the final project."

"Professor, why can't we use these?" Melody asked. "We worked hard on them."

"You've noticed the sketches displayed around the room and know that they are all of Mrs. Hirt, correct? Those are the sketches from last year's final project. I retain the sketches for the next year's class to see. Part of the project is that everyone uses the same model and works on discovering something unique in her. I'm going to cover that with the rest of the class in a few minutes. The assignment due today was for a concept sketch, not a finished drawing. Next week, we will have the model here for each student to set an appointment to sketch. You pose the model for your work, have fifteen minutes to complete your sketch, and then the next student steps in. I'll accept these as concept sketches from you, even though they are way too polished to qualify."

"Oh." There really wasn't much else we could say. We *had* been told to bring a concept sketch for the class. I could just imagine trying to pose old man Johnson on the sofa with a bunch of grapes if he was our required model.

"Now come join the rest of the class. I'll make the full announcement."

———◁◆▷———

"CAN YOU BELIEVE she's coming back? This will be so cool!" Amy practically screamed as we walked to lunch."

"I know you two like her. She really is like your friend, isn't she, Tony?" asked Sandra.

"Well, yeah. We play racquetball."

"She's teaching me," Melody put in. In fact, we had a session with her scheduled this afternoon. I had to admit that I was looking forward to seeing her naked on the model dais again. Of course, this time I had something more tangible to compare her to. Melody and I had been in each other's bed at every opportunity this week and were looking forward to the weekend, even though we both had a crazy lot of homework to do before midterms.

"How'd you guys get into that club?" Amy asked. "I heard it was pretty exclusive." *Pricey*, I thought.

"My dad thought I needed more exercise," I confessed. "I was pretty much a wreck first semester. I guess it did help."

"So what's the story with you two?"

"Sandra!"

"Oh hush, Amy. You know that's the question you really meant to ask. Every time we see Tony or Melody this week, we see Tony *and* Melody. Are you two a couple now?" We looked at each other. We weren't really hiding it, but now we were going to openly declare it.

"Umm… yeah. I guess so."

"Damn, Melody. How'd you get so lucky? I had my eye on Tony!" Sandra said. I nearly spit Coke out my nose, but before I could respond, Amy was echoing almost the same words.

"Damn, Tony. How'd you get so lucky? I had my eye on Melody!" Melody wasn't able to prevent choking on the burger she was eating. It took us a minute to make sure she was okay before both Sandra and Amy burst out laughing.

"Got 'em!" They chorused and high-fived each other. We blushed, I guess. But I wasn't about to let them get away clean with this. I turned and planted a sizzling kiss on Melody that took her so much by surprise she kept her eyes wide open staring at me through the whole thing. It didn't stop her from returning the fervor, though. When we parted from each other, I turned to the other two.

"Eat your hearts out, girls!"

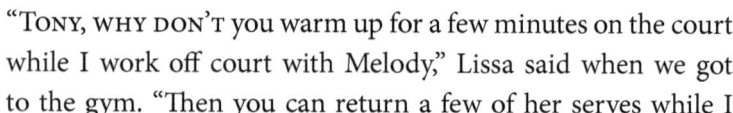

"Tony, why don't you warm up for a few minutes on the court while I work off court with Melody," Lissa said when we got to the gym. "Then you can return a few of her serves while I coach."

I don't know if you've played racquetball. It's not all that uncommon to warm up or to practice alone, even though typically there are two people and sometimes even four on the court for matches. They play doubles racquetball, too, and it can get pretty dangerous with four people swinging racquets around in such a small space. But I really enjoyed my alone time on the court. After I warmed up a little, I started really getting into the groove of firing the ball into the wall, over and over again. When I was really depressed, I'd sometimes work so hard on the court that I could hardly move when I left.

Getting laid regularly was a great antidepressant, but it put a real crimp in study time and I was falling even further behind in a couple of classes. Added to that, it was downright crappy that we wouldn't be able to use the pictures we'd painted for our final. It really pissed me off, even though Melody and I wouldn't have had the incentive to get together last weekend if we hadn't jumped the gun—and each other.

I kept beating the ball harder and harder and sweat started dripping off me as I thought about it. It just… Made me… So… Damn… Mad… that we couldn't use our paintings for the class. It was just another thing that was wrong with college. My favorite class and I'd fucked it up, too. I'd never been punished for working ahead before.

The ball finally got away from me and I turned to retrieve it. Outside the glass back wall, Melody and Lissa were watching me. Melody had her mouth absolutely hanging open. Lissa had a puzzled look on her face, but moved to open the little door to come onto the court.

"Is it safe?"

"Um… yeah. I was… just… warming up." I was drenched in sweat, dripping off my nose onto the floor and panting so hard I couldn't speak. Lissa tossed me a towel. I wiped down and then looked around the floor to mop up any puddles that might make it slippery.

"I'm kinda glad I wasn't in here to take that ass-whipping you just delivered. What got into you?"

"I was just a little frustrated. Sorry."

Melody poked her head into the court.

"Can I come in?" I motioned her in and she came straight up to me and kissed me. It wasn't a big passionate kiss, but it was nice. Real nice. "Ew! You are soaked. I didn't know you could play this by yourself."

"Like many things, you can do it alone but it's a lot better with two. Or three." Lissa said. I glanced at her and she was smiling smugly at her intended suggestive remark. I wasn't sure Melody got it. "Tell me about what's got you so upset, Tony." I leaned back against the wall and slid down it until I was sitting on the floor. I groaned. Lissa and Melody camped right next to me. We had the court reserved. There was nothing in the rules that said we couldn't have a break while we weren't playing. So I started by saying that I was mad because we couldn't use the paintings we'd done of each other. I don't know why, but suddenly everything came unplugged and I just poured out all my frustration with school, my classes, my life, and the failed project. To their credit, neither Melody or Lissa interrupted me or made any attempt to cut me off until I'd vented everything. When I finally wound down, I saw that Melody had tears running down her cheeks and I was struck with sudden pangs of guilt for being so upset when everything between us was so good.

"Tony, have you talked to a school counselor or any of your professors about this?" Lissa asked.

"What could they do? It's my problem. I made a mistake coming here. They can't solve it for me."

"So you figure you have to face everything alone?"

"I'm nineteen. I'm supposed to be an adult."

"So *that's* the magic age! I missed it." Melody and I both looked at Lissa trying to figure out what she was talking about. "I think I skipped nineteen. I'd been on the road as a model for six years and before I was nineteen I had a baby. I never did get to the point where I felt like I was an adult and could solve my own problems. I always had to have someone help me."

"On the road?" Melody asked.

"Lissa, you're an adult. You're married and have kids and everything."

"I have two great kids and an ex-husband. I also have a good shrink who listens to me for an hour a week while I dump out my frustrations, and a racquetball partner who bears the brunt of my physical outbursts on the court. That's you, by the way, in case you were looking for someone else. Even when my marriage was falling apart, though, there were people around that I could talk to who helped me through, whether it was watching the kids, referring me to a good lawyer, or even making my travel arrangements. I never became an adult who could do everything by herself. I really admire you, Tony."

"Even I can tell that was sarcastic," I mumbled.

"Don't you like what *we've* got, Tony?" Melody's voice was scarcely above a whisper, but in the straight-walled enclosure of the court it echoed—or maybe it was only in my head that it was echoing.

"I love what we've got, Melody. This week has been the brightest spot in my entire year—my life—until our meeting with Professor McIntyre today. Then I felt like I was a naughty little boy being disciplined by the teacher. And... well, I guess I'm not really sure *what* we've got. Don't get me wrong. I love the um..." I glanced at Lissa. "You know."

"Sex," Lissa supplied.

"Um... yeah. But I don't know what kind of relationship we have. We haven't really talked a lot about that."

"We've kind of had other things to do when we get together."

"Sex," Lissa repeated.

We finally both looked at her and giggled.

"Yeah. Really, really great..."

"Sex." Melody finished my sentence. We all laughed. Man it felt good just to get all that out and talk about what's going on.

"All right, look, you two. First off, nothing ever gets better all at one time, but it does get better. Sex is great. In fact, it's better than great. But Melody, did you even know Tony was feeling like this?" Melody shook her head. "You guys need to talk some besides jumping each other."

"We have so little time together," I complained.

"All the more reason to use some of it to connect in some way other than genitally. Don't get me wrong. You're probably both getting a lot of comfort and relief from sex, but it might be *increasing* your stress level, too. If you think you might want more than sex later, you'd better find out if you both have the same expectations. Otherwise, I give this about a week more, tops."

"Geez, are you a psychiatrist, Lissa?"

"No."

"What *do* you do?" Melody asked. I think she was trying to give us a break from the intensity of our discussion. It worked and I appreciated it.

"I'm a fashion buyer at Forever Lilly."

"The clothing chain? Wow!"

"It's really not as glamorous as it sounds, but it is pretty fun. It's where models go when they can't make it on the runway anymore."

"I knew modeling for our class wasn't the first time you've modeled."

"No, though usually I had to 'work the dress'. It's a little different when you don't have clothes on, but not much. At one time, Playboy would have paid a bundle for photos of what you've been drawing."

"I bet they still would," I said. Melody looked at me and I could feel myself turn red.

"That was a long time ago. I married my agent when I was eighteen, was a mother when I was nineteen, and by the time I divorced four years later, I had a house, two kids, and depression. I needed some serious help getting my life together."

"But that means you're only, like, not even thirty! I thought you were a lot older," I blurted out. Lissa frowned at me.

"Thanks. I think. Do I look like an old lady to you?"

"No! You just act so mature and you've accomplished so much," Melody helped me out.

"And you used to be the Senior Women's Racquetball Champion."

"Well, I don't know where you got the 'senior' part. I'm only twenty-six. Or 'used to be'. I'm the current Women's Open National Champion. I won it in October. I just don't make a big deal about it."

"Why do you even bother to play with kids like me?" I asked.

"Tony, I like playing with you. A lot. You're fast, energetic, and dedicated. You've got spin that I don't see among most of my competitors. I should ask *you* why you aren't competing."

"Like I'd stand up against that kind of heat. I can't even beat you."

"Bet you could beat everyone else who plays here, though," Lissa said. "Think about it. Who do you lose to at this club besides me? No one. You're the best training competition I can get here."

"Wow, Tony! That's so cool. I knew you were good, but I didn't know you were *that* good."

"If you had any doubts, that last solo skirmish should have canceled them. Melody, you might not know how hard it is to return your own kill shots. Tony kept that ball flying for about thirty volleys. And it just kept going faster. I'm serious. You'd wipe me up if you played like that against me, Tony."

"Thank you, guys," I said. "That makes me feel better about everything but school. But it's a lot." Between exhaustion from my workout and being drained from venting, I was beginning to sag.

"Our court time is about up," Lissa said. "Tell you what. You go relax in the hot tub and I'll go try to seduce your girlfriend since she got to you before I did. Sounds like a fair trade, doesn't it?" Melody's eyes popped open like she'd lose her eyeballs and I got an instant stiffening in my shorts. "Look, Melody," she said, leaning over to blow in her ear. "I think he kind of likes that idea. You've got a kinky boyfriend, lucky girl." Melody looked at me and I saw a smile creep across her face as she pointedly looked at my crotch. Then she did what neither Lissa nor I expected. She turned and planted a smoldering kiss on our racquetball mentor.

"Oh, my! I need a shower," she said as she stood up. We all got up to leave and I noticed the two guys standing outside waiting for their court time. As we left the court they grinned at us. It took a long time in the steam room before I remembered to be depressed.

Wait! Lissa complained that Melody got to me before she did?

FIVE

T**HE NEXT WEEK** was just as tough as the previous week was, but Melody and I managed some quality time where we actually talked to each other instead of trying to devour each other. And we got some of the other kind of quality time, too, though not anywhere near what we wanted. Midterms were in two weeks and the profs were really loading on the work. It seemed like we had to cover twice as much in art history in half the time. There were midterm papers due soon for four classes.

Lissa asked us to spend the next weekend with her and I just had to ask Melody about the kiss. It was so hot and it kept replaying in my mind.

"So what kind of experience did you have before you gave me your virginity?" Melody asked.

"Five fingers and a little groping on a hot date," I answered truthfully.

"Yeah. Pretty much me too, though I'd had a little girl-girl action. Just like kissing and touching stuff. I've always known I was equally attracted to men and women. I hope you don't find that offensive. Don't you wonder what other experiences are out there? Don't get me wrong. I love sex with you. I think I love you, but don't hold me to that yet. The thing is, I… we don't know beans about 90% of sex."

"If what we've got is only 10%, I'm sure the rest would kill me!"

"It'd be fun to try, though, wouldn't it? You see... oh geez... that kiss with Lissa? It wasn't the first time."

"The first time you kissed a girl?"

"The first time I kissed Lissa. When I first thought about seducing you, I considered inviting Sandra or Amy to help, but I don't trust them exactly. With Lissa? Can *you* trust her?" I raised an eyebrow, a little worried. "Don't panic. She's missing some vital equipment. But still... can't you just imagine us all together?"

I couldn't deny that the idea of *anything* with Lissa turned me on. I'd probably had more fantasies about her than anyone I'd met in the past year, and when you tossed Melody into the mix, the possibilities seemed endless.

"I've thought about the two of you together in the spa a few times," I admitted. "Are you seriously suggesting... Like the three of us? You think she'd...? Really? You'd be cool with that?"

"She invited us to her house this weekend. She says the kids will be with their dad and we could come and... I think she said, 'sketch to our hearts' content', if I remember the exact words. Did you think she meant landscapes?"

"I thought maybe she was just giving us a chance to be together."

"She is. All three of us."

———⋘✦⋙———

FRIDAY WAS A tough day for Lissa. She was an experienced runway model, but posing without moving is hard work. Every student in the class got to pose her and do a fifteen-minute sketch. She got a fifteen-minute break every hour. That meant she worked from 9:00 in the morning until 4:30 in the afternoon with only a slightly longer break for lunch. Melody and I had the last two timeslots on the schedule and Lissa sighed when I moved my easel to the center spot. All the other students except Melody had left. Even Professor McIntyre had left and told me to turn out the lights when we were through. Normal rules say that a model has to put on her robe during breaks, but as we were setting up, Lissa just stood there looking at us. I guess I was looking at her, too.

"Why don't you two do your sketches at my place?" she asked. "There's really no reason for us to stay here any longer, is there?" Melody nodded and we grabbed our easels and equipment while Lissa dressed. "My car is at the loading dock," Lissa said. "They gave me a special permit for the day." When we got downstairs, the car was the same burgundy Mazda SUV that Melody had driven two weeks ago. Lissa unlocked it and as we loaded our gear. I shot a quizzical look at Melody.

"Whose house did you think we were at?" she asked.

"I didn't know. I thought it was just a friend of yours."

"Yeah, well, it is."

Lissa's house was just as I remembered it. In fact, our props were still set up in the lower level. We set up our easels, lights, drapes, and paints.

"Guys, do you mind if we don't start working right away?" Lissa asked. She'd watched the setup, but she definitely looked tired. "That was a long day and I could really use a nice long soak and a glass of wine. Want to join me?"

"Where? I didn't know you had a hot tub."

"Jacuzzi in the master bath. I take it you two never made it to that room when you were here."

"Never even occurred to us," Melody said. "We were kind of occupied."

We went to the kitchen and Lissa handed me a bottle of white wine and a corkscrew. I looked at them and decided I could figure it out. I'd never opened a bottle of wine that had a cork. She handed Melody a tray of cheese and crackers that was already on the counter to warm up to room temperature and then reached for a bowl of grapes. She turned to me.

"Are we going to need all of these for your sketch?"

"Um… no. Just one medium bunch." I reached over and used the kitchen scissors on the counter to cut a section apart from the rest and Lissa put it on a plate in the fridge. She brought the rest with her as she led us to her bedroom.

I was raised to respect people's privacy, so it really hadn't occurred to me to open the door to the master bedroom when we'd visited two weeks ago. If I had, I'd have realized right away that it was Lissa's house. There were pictures of her and her kids all over the room. It was such a complete difference from the rest of the house that was sparsely decorated with art pieces and modern furniture. This looked like a Victorian bedroom and sitting room. It even had a fireplace in one corner and a huge high bed that dominated the main room.

"I pretty much live in the master suite," Lissa said. "The boys love to play all over the house, but when they go away for the weekend, everything goes back into their room and the rest of the house is just for show."

"This is beautiful," Melody said. Lissa lit the sitting room fireplace and stepped into the bathroom. The fireplace was two-sided so the gas fire could be seen from both the sitting/ dressing area and the huge marble tub and shower in the bathroom. Lissa continued moving around the bathroom, lighting candles and filling the tub. She set the wine, cheeses, and grapes around the foot-and-a-half wide tub edge and turned to smile at us.

"Well, don't just stand there," she said. "Let's enjoy it." With that she casually slipped out of her blouse and skirt. Artist models are allowed privacy to dress and undress. They approach the dais with a robe on, get in position and then hand the robe to the instructor. Students *never* watch the model undress. I was dumbstruck watching Lissa slip out of real clothes, realizing for the first time that she wasn't posing as a model, she was undressing for me... us. Melody nudged me and I was suddenly aware that I was the only one in the room with clothes on. I undressed. At least it wasn't a stubby little dick that I'd be embarrassed about. Geez. Isn't there some stage between nonexistent and raging hard-on?

We all three stepped into the spa. The tub was so big we probably could have put three more in it.

"This is so nice," Lissa said, leaning back with just her chin and head above water. I caught another glimpse of her nipples as they rose above the water just before the jets kicked in and bubbles covered us all. "I hardly ever use this because it's so big. I'm afraid I'd drown in it and no one would ever know." She poured a little wine for each of us and handed us the glasses, then raised them in a toast. "Here is to a relaxing weekend filled with art, music, and friends. May it be a time of discovery." We clinked our glasses and had a sip of the wine.

For a while we just sat in the tub together unwinding and eating. As our legs relaxed, our feet and ankles touched and then more of our legs wound together. In the process, we all ended up lying in the tub next to each other with me in the middle. Melody snuggled up to my left and I wrapped my arm around her. Her breasts against my wet skin felt so delicious. Lissa looked across me to her and raised an eyebrow.

Melody nodded her head as their silent communication continued. Lissa slid against me in exactly the same position on my right side and her hard nipples raked against my chest. She turned her head and kissed my shoulder. At the same time, Melody raised her lips and nibbled on my earlobe. I squeezed both ladies in a hug. I was in heaven. The slight pressure and the way their buoyant bodies were bounced around by the jets pushed them both toward the center and they looked at each other for a few seconds before moving their heads together for a kiss. I could see it was just lips for a bit, but as they continued Lissa sucked gently at Melody's lower lip and then slipped her tongue across it. I could see Melody's tongue thrust toward our friend and make contact. It was so hot to watch them kissing while using my chest as a pillow that I almost burst.

"Oh!" I groaned. Two hands reached my cock at the same time and gently stroked up and down. There was little I could do to respond since I had an arm trapped behind each woman. As if they were communicating through their tongues, both lifted up until their lips were even with mine. With only a slight turn of their heads, we were all three included in the kiss.

A three-way kiss can simply be a tangle of noses and cheekbones. But if you are as relaxed as we were, it just sort of works out. They were anchored to the center by their grip on my cock and my hands could drift down their backs to caress their beautiful asses. Lissa's favorite move was sucking my lower lip and pulling it back. That exposed interesting contact points as Melody ran her tongue along the inner lip and my teeth. Then I nipped Lissa's upper lip with my teeth and felt Melody's tongue slide into our friend's mouth. We just kissed like that forever. Sometimes two would become deeply passionate while the third rained light kisses over their cheeks and eyes. Sometimes all three would meet for a midair tongue battle. We rubbed noses, cheeks, and even fluttered our eyelashes across an exposed neck or raised chin. We parted, looked into our partners' eyes and then moved back together. We were making love to each other without ever having intercourse. But somehow, I suspected that would work out as well.

The water was actually beginning to cool a little and we were getting shriveled. At least parts of us were. They let go of my cock and rolled off me. That finally gave me access to put my hands in more interesting places and both seemed willing to let me explore their bodies. I couldn't help but compare Lissa's slightly larger firmer breasts to Melody's exquisite softness, right up to the points of her nipples. When my hands slid down their stomachs and I felt the smooth shape of their pussies, Lissa stood up.

"Come on, you two. The water's getting cold." She stepped out of the tub and grabbed three towels off a rack. They were warm and fluffy. I started to dry myself off, but Lissa put a stop to that. "I didn't give you *your* towel," she grinned. I got the idea and reached out with the towel I was holding to dry her. Lissa started drying Melody and I felt Melody pat me dry with the towel she held. It was a tangle of arms, legs, and towels as we each tried to get someone else dry. We ended up giggling like crazy as we followed Lissa toward her huge bed. She pulled the covers down and we all tumbled in, still playing and tickling one another.

SIX

MELODY LANDED in the middle. Both Lissa and I were stroking her body and massaging her breasts.

"Take it easy there, stud," Lissa said. "Have you asked how Melody likes to have her breasts played with? How about it, Mel? Do you like rough stuff or a lighter touch?" Melody's eyes flicked open and looked at us.

"Gosh. I never thought about the differences. I like it when Tony touches me, but sometimes it *is* a little rough."

"You have to tell him what you like."

"Um… I like it when you do that kind of feathery touch where you just run your fingers over my breasts. It makes me feel all gooey."

"Like this?" Lissa demonstrated and I recognized that I'd done that once or twice, but I didn't realize how much Melody liked it. I copied the moves as I saw Lissa do them and Melody squirmed on the bed.

"Oh! Oh, I like that! I like it because I just know that at any moment you'll brush up against my nipple, but I don't know when. The suspense is killing me." Lissa grinned at me and I copied her as she started at the bottom of Melody's breast and began lightly spiraling upward toward the tip. Just before she reached the pink areola, though, she let her fingers glide back down. I chased them with my hand off the other breast and we both ended up gliding across her pubic bone and then circling back up toward her delectable orbs. Melody was going crazy. Our hands crossed and this time I circled the breast closest to Lissa and she caressed the one closest to me. I noticed with pleasure that when I circled Melody's breast, the back of my hand brushed against Lissa's breast and she caught her breath. She smiled at me and circled around Melody's breast again so that when I copied her I brushed across her nipple again. This time, instead of tracing down her stomach, we crossed between the breasts and up on the other side. Melody moaned out, "please."

Lissa smiled at me again and positioned her hand so that her fingertips and thumb were spread around the breast, but the palm wasn't touching. When she saw that I'd copied the position, she began to draw the fingers up toward the nipple, finally sliding across the areola and just before we reached the tips of her nipples, squeezing just a little and letting go completely. Melody gasped. Her body went rigid and her butt lifted up off the bed. "Ohhhhh! Oh god! Oh. You… You just made me come without even touching my clit. You only… you barely touched my nipples. Oh god!"

"Pleasure for a woman isn't a formula, Tony. You can't just do what you did last time and expect the same result. You mix the game up a little bit, find out what is pleasing to your partner, and then let the tension build until she explodes." I'd have answered her, but Melody had grabbed the back of my head and pulled it down for a hot, searing kiss. As soon as she let me go, she pulled Lissa to her and gave her some of the same.

"Thank you. Thank you so much."

"Are you all satisfied now?" Lissa asked.

"You aren't going to stop, are you? No, I'm not satisfied. I want more!" Melody said.

Lissa laughed.

"Isn't that what you want to hear from your lover, Tony? 'More. I want more?' Most women can climax several times to each time a man comes. Maybe not every time, but often. When she wants more, you want to be able to give her more. So you have to use everything you've got to please her.

"Your lips." Lissa stroked a finger across my lips and it sent shivers down my spine.

"Your tongue." She said that just as my tongue darted out of my mouth to lick her finger. It was like a reflex. She dragged her finger down my chin, my throat, and my chest until she circled my nipple, then flicked back up across my shoulder and down my arm to my hand.

"Your fingers." Her hand continued, sliding down my leg and then back up the inside of my thigh to circle my balls and stroke slowly up…

"Your cock." I shuddered and took a deep breath. Melody responded the same way. I looked at her and her eyes were glassy and unfocused as she listened intently to every word Lissa said. My cock, as it happened, was only inches away from Melody's pussy and Lissa crossed from my body to hers in one unhurried stroke from the middle of her thighs up to Melody's parted labia.

"Even your voice," Lissa whispered. Melody jumped straight into the air as Lissa stroked once across her clit. She cried out in orgasm, panting for breath.

"Are you satisfied now, Little One?"

"N… no. I… want… more."

"I'm so happy to hear that." Lissa parted Melody's legs and the two of us lay side-by-side between them staring up into Melody's wide open pussy. "Did you know Latin is the foundation of all Romance languages? Repeat after me," Lissa instructed as she began pointing out the features of what we were looking at. "The pudenda, also called the vulva. Mons pubis. Labia majora. Labia minora. Vestibule. Introitus. Clitoris. Perineum. Anus." I repeated each word as Lissa's fingers outlined each part of Melody's sex. "All can be stimulated. Now here is one more Latin word." Lissa leaned forward and ran her tongue all the way from Melody's anus to her clitoris and back.

"Oh yes, oh yes, oh yes. That feels so good!"

"Cunnilingus," Lissa whispered. She moved aside far enough that I could repeat the gesture with my tongue and repeat the word back to her.

"Cunnilingus."

Melody had pulled her legs up and back to open herself as widely as she could and give us both access. I stayed focused on what Lissa was doing with her tongue and each time she showed me a way to stimulate some part of Melody, I repeated the gesture. Melody was writhing on the bed, gasping out incoherent words and phrases as she came repeatedly. Then Lissa backed away just as far as my ear so she could continue to whisper instructions as I continued to bathe Melody with my tongue.

"Your tongue in her vagina. Circle her clitoris but don't press down on it. Suck the outer labia. Tickle the anus. Finger on perineum while you tongue vagina. Light stroke of thumb on anus while your finger slides into her vagina. Suck her clitoris and flick the tip with your tongue. Flatten your tongue against her clitoris as your finger slips into her vagina. Curl your finger upward and vibrate it lightly behind the urethra. Shake your head a little."

That did it. Melody's legs shot out straight as she screamed. For a minute, Lissa and I were both trapped beneath her legs as she tried desperately to squeeze them together around both of us. Her pussy was drenched in juices that ran down my lips and chin. If Lissa had neighbors nearby, I'm sure they would have called the police. Just when I thought Melody was finished and her legs were relaxing, I guess I let my tongue flick her clit one more time and she screamed again.

When Melody finally relaxed enough for us to move, Lissa and I rolled onto our sides with our cheeks resting on Melody's mound. Lissa kissed me and licked Melody's juices off my face. My cock was pressed between her legs and I could feel her hand stroking my balls. I desperately wanted to fuck her and nudged forward. Lissa pulled back enough to signal me to wait. It was hard, but I did as she said, holding still with my cock poised at her moist entrance.

"Little One? Are you satisfied?" There was a long silence and I thought maybe Melody had gone to sleep. I couldn't really see more than her chin as I looked up between her beautiful breasts. Then I heard the whisper.

"N... nn... no? M... m... more, please?" My god, she could hardly speak and she was still asking for more. Lissa smiled at me and moved away. She guided me by the cock until I crawled up above Melody. Lissa positioned my cock at Melody's pussy and slowly guided me in. The growl in Melody's throat started low and increased until I was fully buried. Then her eyes snapped open and locked on mine. Her arms wrapped around me and pulled me tight against her body.

"Ohhh! God!!! I love you, Tony!" She hauled my face to hers and kissed me with such passion that I stopped breathing. I could feel my heart pounding in every extremity of my body and it was matched beat for beat with hers where we were joined. I knew I was close, but I had to satisfy Melody. I *needed* to satisfy her. I pulled back and thrust in again. One more time and Melody erupted. I could feel every muscle in her vagina as it clamped down on me. At the same time, I felt Lissa's fingers press in beneath my balls and I exploded with such force I was sure I would pass out.

"Melody! I… Love… You!" I shouted out as every spurt from my cock was matched by a convulsion in her pussy. When I finally remembered to breathe again, I rolled to the side and brought Melody with me so we were facing each other. I felt Lissa crawl up, hauling the covers over the three of us as we lay there. I was sandwiched again between Melody and Lissa with my cock still inside. Melody looked over my shoulder and I could feel Lissa's lips there as they kissed.

"Satisfied," Melody whispered. She closed her eyes and we all drifted off to sleep.

———◁◆▷———

WHEN MELODY AND I awoke in the morning, we were lying side-by-side, no longer connected as we were when we went to sleep, but pressing together, nonetheless. Lissa wasn't in bed with us. We could smell coffee and hear her moving in the kitchen.

"Thank you for last night," Melody said as she kissed me softly.

"It was wonderful," I said.

"Did you… did you mean it?" she asked, suddenly unable to meet my eyes. I thought back. It's one thing to tell a woman you love her when you're blasting your semen deep inside her. But in the light of day? The next morning? It dawned on me that I wasn't depressed this morning. In fact, I felt better than I had in months. I smiled and lifted her chin so she could look me in the eye again.

"Yes. I love you, Melody." She didn't answer with words.

—————◁◆▷—————

WE WERE ALL downstairs in our makeshift studio. None of us bothered to put clothes on after we woke up. We all showered together and this time took turns toweling one another dry so it wasn't quite the mass confusion of limbs and towels it was the night before. We were all relaxed. Somehow, being constantly in the presence of these two incredible women, my cock kept going from half-mast to full-mast, but never shriveled to its customary peanut size. Melody won the toss, so Lissa posed for her first. The pose was almost exactly the same as I posed two weeks ago. I could see as she worked that this sketch was far superior to the one of me. Maybe we'd been a little too focused on hurrying our sketches so we could fuck some more. Melody's style was simple and bold. She captured the cat in Lissa. The tension was there. The grace was there. The power was there. Even her facial expression was somehow feral. We had the leisure to work a little longer on each sketch than we would have had in class and Lissa held the pose for longer than we ever normally ask of a model.

When Melody was finished with the sketch, Lissa relaxed and stretched her back and shoulders. She came over to look at Melody's drawing. As we admired her work, I reached up and started massaging Lissa's shoulders. We'd worked on each other a little after matches and I knew she liked to have me dig my thumbs into her traps and delts. At the club, though, she'd be wearing a shirt and bra. She was purring and leaned her bare back into me as she talked to Melody about the drawing. My cock was rock hard against Lissa's ass, just from giving her a little massage. Lissa squeezed her cheeks together around my trapped cock. Melody looked up at us and smiled. She reached over and began working on Lissa's left leg. This was no playful stroking, but some serious massage. Lissa was tight as a drum and after about ten minutes with her leaning against me and being rubbed by the two of us, she was beginning to melt.

I went to the kitchen to get her a bottle of water. When I got back, Melody and Lissa were in front of my setting looking at the drawings I'd done of Melody two weeks ago. I could just see Lissa positioning herself as she looked at the drawing. She raised a hand above her head, then looked at the setting and switched hands. She twisted a little one way, then the other.

When Lissa had finished her water and was ready to go back to work, we talked about the pose and what I wanted to capture.

"I think I've got the body position down," Lissa said. "But there's something…" She went over to stand in front of the daybed. She looked at it, repositioned a pillow slightly and turned back toward us. "I think you are going to have to show me *exactly* how you got that expression on her face."

I looked at Melody and she grinned at me. I smiled.

"It will take a little time, but I think we can put that smile on your face," I said. Lissa bit her lower lip coyly. Melody and I advanced on her.

We had all weekend for sketching.

SEVEN

MONDAY WAS a great day. After a weekend spent with two incredible women who both wanted to take regular play breaks, I was so sexually sated and so much in love that I could hardly stand it. Of course, Melody and I both had to stay up most of Sunday night doing the projects that were due for classes on Monday morning, but that's college life. Half the dorm was up all night doing the same thing.

The downside was that I was so tired by Monday evening that when I went to the club to play racquetball, I got totally smeared by a guy I'd beaten in straight sets three weeks ago. Even my serves were off and I fouled away the final point. I fell into bed Monday night and almost missed my first class on Tuesday by the time I woke up.

That was a great start to Tuesday. Not to mention the fact that in Fundamentals we spent three hours sizing canvases. It's messy. That spray starch from Magic or Niagara doesn't come close to getting your hands in and painting a coat of what amounts gooey glue on a canvas that is thirty feet wide and fifteen feet deep that will be used for a theater backdrop. And you can't just throw the stuff at the canvas because if it isn't in a smooth, even coat, you can get lumps and sags. All I wanted after class was a hot shower, but of course I had to go to Art Orientation immediately after I got out of Fundamentals and barely had time for lunch, let alone a shower. I usually tried to play racquetball on Tuesday, but I had a massive paper describing the transition from Realism to Impressionism and what influences were at play due for Art History on Wednesday. I made a quick call to the gym and rescheduled my court time for Wednesday afternoon instead. Phil might be pissed, but you could almost always pick up a new partner if one flaked out.

I got to bed again and didn't sleep well because I didn't have any exercise during the day, except for my right arm, which was sore because I was wielding an eight-inch brush heavy with flex glue all morning. And what did I care anyway because school was a shitbag and I'd never pass this semester anyway. I didn't know why I was here in the first place. Even when Melody caught up with me after dinner, she said I smelled so bad that I should really consider clean clothes tomorrow. She barely pecked me on the cheek and said she had to go study something for her Textiles class. I hated this school and I didn't really care if everyone knew it. Yeah, I know. *Whine, whine, whine. What a pussy.* It seemed like I simply couldn't control my life or my emotions or even carve out time to connect with my lover. Lovers. Even my love life was confusing. When was I going to see Lissa again?

I dropped my paper in the basket at the door of the auditorium where Dr. Bychkova was about to lecture to yet another sleeping class. I'd just settled into my seat when the TA announced over the PA that I was supposed to report to the Dean's office immediately after class. Of course he had to announce it over the PA because he didn't have the foggiest idea who I was, so half a dozen kids who do know me swiveled in their seats to stare at me and raise eyebrows as if to ask me what was up. That movement near me caused the rest of the class to turn and stare to see who the dunce was that got called to the principal's office. I felt like I was in third grade and it completely ruined the nap during Bychkova's lecture.

———◁◆▷———

WHEN I WALKED into Dean Peterson's office and told his admin, Miss Stevenson, that I'd been summoned, she motioned me to a seat and I found there were four other students sitting waiting as well.

"I'm sorry," Dean Peterson said when he came out of his office. "I was going to do this all at once, but I've decided I need to speak to each of you individually. Jason Roe?" A guy sitting next to me stood up and went with the Dean. My stomach growled, but it was a cinch I wasn't going to get any lunch again today. I sniffed at my clothes—thankfully I'd found something fairly clean to wear today—thinking I might not make it to Visual Concepts. Ms. Brockman wouldn't be happy about that.

It took almost an hour for Dean Peterson to get through the others sitting in the office. Napping in the waiting room wasn't as comfortable as the seats in the auditorium. The secretary had taken down our names as we came in, so I was sitting there last as everybody else walked out. At least they didn't look like they were being expelled. In fact, most of them had a kind of vacant, daydreaming look on their faces.

"Tony, at last," Dr. Peterson said when I walked in. "I'm sorry it took so long to process the others, but I wanted to spend some time with you anyway. I'll make sure Ms. Brockman understands that your absence is my fault."

He looked at me as though he expected me to say something. I had no idea what. I just said, "Okay."

Mural

The Dean sorted through some papers, setting aside two folders. That left just one on his desk. I assumed it was mine. How could the school compile a folder that thick on me in just one and a half semesters?

"How are you doing, Tony?" What the hell did he want me to say?

"Um… okay." Boy I was being creative in my responses.

"I deserved that. You really don't know me from Adam and I ask a question expecting you to be forthright and revealing about yourself. Forget I asked it. Let me start over." I was about to say okay again, but I decided I'd better not push it.

"We're a small school. Still, when a student comes here, it's just as likely that he feels as lost and alone as he would at a big university. The difference is that the faculty here actually know their students. Of course there are a few big general classes, but aside from Art History, what is the biggest class you have?"

"You mean number of students? Uh… about twenty-five, I guess." Boy, was I a wordsmith today!

"Right. It might surprise you to know that each of your professors actually knows your name and how you are doing." I laughed nervously. "What?"

"It's hard to imagine that Dr. Bychkova even knows there is a class in the auditorium when he lectures."

"Yes. Well, there *are* exceptions. And I already pointed out his class as an exception to class size. But in this case, even Dr. Bychkova has supplied me with a report on your progress." I gulped. I didn't think I'd screwed anything up too bad in Art History. And did that mean all my profs supplied some report to the Dean? *Shit!*

"Your instructors speak highly of you, Tony. But they all seem to think you are unhappy here. Your work doesn't live up to what they see as your ability. They see you get inspired with something and do work that is outstanding, but that your daily work is average. I know you are an artist, Tony, but you can't work solely from inspiration. What do you see as the problem?"

"It's boring. I swung an eight-inch paint brush for three hours yesterday loaded with flex glue. Three hours painting a house would have been more profitable."

"Yes. That's a cost of a fine arts education. There's a lot of work that goes into operating a studio and someone has to do it. I'm sure you would find the same attitude among the theater techs, the graphic arts students, and even the dancers. In order to have painted sets, you have to have stretched canvases for the backdrops. In order to paint those canvases, you have to have them sized. It is part of being an artist, even if it is a boring and tedious part. It's like playing scales on the piano."

"But that's not fair. There's no intellectual challenge here. It's like just because we are artists, we're not supposed to read or do math. It makes it feel like getting a BFA is just for kids who can't cut studying. Even the homework we have for most classes just involves more sweeping floors. We might as well get a degree in auto mechanics or better yet, street paving." *Wow! Did I just tell the Dean that I thought the degree I was aspiring to was worthless? Yeah. I guess I did. Fuck.*

"Good point. And, in general, your professors agree. Especially about you. You are a talented artist, but your mind is turning to mush." This was it, I thought. Now he was going to tell me that I should leave. Well, that was fine. I was going to leave at the end of the semester anyway.

"Are you familiar with Seattle Cascades University?" Dr. Peterson asked.

"Just that it's another college a few blocks from here. Seems like there are colleges all over this city."

"Actually, a pretty good little university. In fact, so good that we've begun exploring a shared curriculum with them. Back in the 70s, there was a big move toward specialization. Although art schools had been around for a while, the fine arts baccalaureate became something to be aspired to. It was a degree for those who would actually become professionals in their field. But academics for those individuals suffered. It seems now that there should be a compromise of some sort. So, we're looking at cross disciplinary studies. Letting humanities students with talent take art classes here, for example. And letting our students with a more academic bent, take classes and even earn a degree from SCU."

"You mean it might be possible to switch to a BA in Art instead of a BFA?" That would answer a problem. Of course, I was pretty sure I'd be accepted on an Art BA at UNeb and not have to move back to depressing Seattle. Depressing except that Melody and Lissa are here. *Damn it! How am I supposed to make this kind of decision?*

"Not quite. SCU doesn't offer a BA in Art. But it does offer a degree in Art and Literary Criticism. Tony, we've got an experimental program we're working on that would provide certain talented students like yourself with double degrees. You could complete your BFA in Studio Art and a BA in… You seem to have a strong interest in literature, right? Or, perhaps you'd like to focus on physical education."

"Yessir. I mean, no sir. You mean I could earn two degrees at the same time?"

"Yes, exactly. We would like to have you be one of the first dozen students who earn double degrees. The program is being offered to select students entering their sophomore year at each school. Specifically, four from each institution. Next year, double that number. It is possible that you would need to take an extra semester or even two to finish, but you would receive a BFA from Pacific College of the Arts and Design, and a BA from Seattle Cascades University, awarded at a joint commencement."

"I can't afford an extra semester," I said. "I don't want to leave school $100,000 in debt."

"Part two of the offer. Full ride for as long as you maintain a 3.0 average. Including room and board. That means you'll have to focus and maintain grades even on the manual labor classes."

"Full ride? That's incredible!"

"Tony, we recruited you to come to our college. I'm pretty sure you think that was to fulfill a quota and have a male painter. We recruited you because we thought you would make a significant contribution to the college, both as a student and as an alumnus. You may not realize it yet, but your professors here at PCAD are watching out for you and have noticed that you are unhappy. After talking to each of them, they have agreed that you are an ideal candidate for this program. What do you think?"

"It sounds too good to be true. I was thinking of transferring out."

"You wouldn't be the first good student we've lost. But we'd like to keep you."

"Can I think about it a little?"

"Of course. I don't expect you to make this big a decision without thinking about it. You might even want to call your parents."

"Thank you, sir."

"There is one more thing."

"Yes sir?"

"I'm informed that you are also an athlete."

"I try to keep it a secret, sir." He actually laughed. I was feeling pretty bold right now since I wasn't being expelled.

"I've often wished we had a sports program here at PCAD. But SCU does have one."

"I play racquetball. It's not exactly an NCAA varsity sport."

"But there is a collegiate conference. Part of the package is an athletic scholarship to play racquetball for SCU, effective immediately. Your current class registrations will be officially transferred to the joint program which would make you eligible for the USAR National Intercollegiate Championships next month."

"SCU has a racquetball team?"

"No. You would be it."

"I'd...?" I didn't even know what kind of question to ask. This was overwhelming.

"I'm sorry. I didn't mean to hold you here so long this afternoon. You've missed most of your Visual Concepts class, so why don't you take off early for the gym. That will be a good place to think things over. Stop by before your first class on Friday and let me know what you're thinking. I'll let you get on to your practice. By the way, if you accept this deal, your court time will be covered by the SCU school athletic committee. Enjoy your exercise, Tony."

I was dismissed. Just like that. I wondered if I walked out of his office with the same dazed look that I'd seen on the faces of those who were before me. I had to close my mouth or I'd be drooling.

How the heck did Dean Peterson know I'd rescheduled my court time for this afternoon?

EIGHT

"**F**ocus!"

Another shot hit me square in the chest as my racquet swished at empty air.

"Get your head in the game or I'm going to put the next one right down your throat." Lissa really growled at me. I'd never seen her so intense. I didn't even expect her to be here today. I don't normally come in on Wednesday. She gave me a wicked serve right back along the wall and it barely touched the floor before it came off the back wall low in the corner.

By some miracle, I caught it with the tip of my racquet and even though it wasn't in the sweet spot, I got enough on the ball to slam it into the end wall without lifting it more than six inches off the floor. This time Lissa growled as she scrambled back to her original spot and slammed the ball back to me again. My head finally snapped into the game and I was just 'there' when the ball came back. I gave it enough back spin on my return that it hit the front wall and died. There was no way Lissa could get to it. She screamed like it was her victory.

"Yes!" I looked at her like she was crazy and the look in her eyes told me she might just be. She set up to serve again without hesitating. I was ready for the heat this time and drove the ball off two corners and down to the floor. She sent it back to me just as hard and I had to take it off the back wall. She spiked. I returned. She came in low and I dropped the ball dead by pulling my racquet back just at the moment I made contact. She dove at the ball and returned it, but it bounced back off the wall and hit her for an interference call. No point.

The rest of the match followed the same pattern. When I had come onto the court, I was still thinking about what the dean had told me. I was surprised to find Lissa there. She said she always played on Wednesdays and snapped me up when my name came up on the rotation. I wasn't doing well processing things for the first several volleys. There was too much going on in my life. I looked at Lissa in a whole new way and she got irritated with me. *God! I was in that gorgeous woman's bed this weekend. In her.*

The last time she yelled at me, somehow it got through to me and suddenly I couldn't see or hear anything but the little blue ball as it flew around the room. I was the ball. It was wherever I was. I simply couldn't miss.

I think it is the first time I ever beat Lissa in a match. And I was sure she hadn't held back. When she called out the final score it didn't even register in my brain that I'd won. When she wrapped her arms around me for a hug, we squished together like a couple of wet sponges. Then it hit me. I'd just won. Man I felt great! I could just do this forever.

WE LEFT THE court and two guys I didn't recognize were standing outside. I hadn't really been aware of them before, but I vaguely remembered seeing them when I went onto the court. They must have watched the whole game. One was wearing the white polo shirt and blue warmup pants of the club trainers. The other was in jeans, but wore a plaid shirt and tie with a corduroy sport coat. Lissa brought me up short as I was headed for the showers by grabbing hold of my arm and hauling me straight in front of the suit.

The guy looked me up and down. I was still breathing pretty hard, but I stood up straight under his scrutiny. I wasn't sure what he was, but he seemed important. The club trainer had a clipboard and they glanced through the notes there and then back up at me.

"What's going on?" I asked. I think I was asking Lissa, but I was looking at these two guys.

"Tony, this is Mr. Jacobson, athletic director at SCU," Lissa said.

"Pleased to meet you, Mr. Jacobson," I said, holding out my hand to shake. He took it and shook it firmly.

"I think you can call me Sam. If all goes well, we'll be seeing a lot of each other. Let me introduce John Gilbert. John is a personal trainer here at the club." We shook hands.

"What's this all about?" I asked. I had a suspicion, but… *Gee!*… I'd only had my conversation with the Dean a couple of hours ago. What was the rush?

"Tony, you talked to Dean Peterson a little while ago. I'm not exactly sure you understood what he was offering you on behalf of both Pacific College of the Arts and Design and Seattle Cascades University. I was sent down to assess your potential for the athletic portion of your scholarship and to discuss your training program. SCU doesn't have a racquetball club yet, so bringing on an athlete in that area is a stretch for us. It means that we don't have coaches or other staff that could help you. And, while you will have access to SCU facilities, we can't really provide training staff in time for you to get ready for this year's competition."

They were really acting like this was all a done deal. An athletic scholarship? For an artist? Get real. I liked racquetball, but it's not a varsity sport. I looked at Lissa and began to shake my head.

"I'm training for a return to Opens in the fall," Lissa said. "The best workout I get is from you. I've agreed to work as your coach for the Intercollegiate in exchange for you helping me get ready to defend my title."

"I don't think I have time for this…"

"We'll talk about your time, Tony," Lissa said, "First listen to the offer. John is my trainer here at the club. He's agreed to take you on as well. The trainer is not the coach. John will get you through three days a week of weight and flexibility training, including Pilates. It does absolute wonders for your reach."

"The weight training is limited," John broke in, "because we don't want to tie up your speed in bulk. It's focused on increasing your power, not building up additional muscle. As for aerobics, you'll get enough of that three days a week when you train with Lissa."

"Three days a week? I'm already fucking overwhelmed with school!" I blurted out. "Now you want to add three more days of training and longer workouts?" I was near tears. The fantasy Dean Peterson painted for me was just that—a fantasy. The reality was just a lot more stress in my life. I turned away. Lissa caught me before I got to the locker room door and caught my arm.

"Just dress and get back out here," she commanded. "We'll shower and take a hot tub at my place."

"I've got homework."

"Bring it with you. I'll help. Pull your head out of your ass and focus on me." I looked up into her intense blue eyes. I was still pissed and felt like shit. But I couldn't look away from her. "We're going to get you through this. We're going to do it together. Tony, this isn't just about you. I don't have a coach and I *need* your help, too. Now get dressed and be out here in five minutes." I just nodded and went into the locker room.

———⧏✦⧐———

"THERE'S THIRTEEN DIFFERENT weights of muslin and canvas, the primary material used in studio and theater," I said. "I'm supposed to have a description of each one and its uses for a class presentation in Fundamentals tomorrow." Lissa was stretched out in the tub next to me. We were both naked, but it wasn't sexual this time. In fact, I was having a hard time even thinking of her sexually. We were sharing a hot tub like any other two athletes would after a match. We each had a large bottle of cold water and were drinking steadily. I sweat so much during a hard workout that I can lose as much as three pounds in water weight. That's three pints of water I need to replenish to avoid dehydration.

"And why have you waited until tonight to start this project?"

"I was kinda busy this weekend."

"God, Tony! You can't blame not getting your homework done on having two insatiably horny women around!" I looked over at Lissa. We held a straight face for almost five seconds before we both spit our drinks out of our mouths and broke down laughing. I laughed so hard it almost felt like an orgasm. I had visions of myself sitting at a desk writing a paper while Melody and Lissa made out naked on top of it. Yeah, sure. I could do that.

I felt so much better after laughing that I just sank down in the tub and laid my head back on the edge.

"What do you like best about school, Tony?"

"Mmmm… I like my girlfriend. And my… um… coach."

"All right. Number one on Tony's 'why I like school' list is sex. We got that. What else."

"I like painting. I mean really painting or even drawing. When I sit down at my easel, or when I pick up a sketch pad, I enter my own world. I could do it forever. That's why I thought I'd like art school. I'd be able to spend all my time in that zone. Like when I sketched you this weekend. I loved all the sexy things we were doing, but when I was sketching, it wasn't sexual. I was lost in the shadows. Did you know that when the light is right, there is a little extra shadow on your throat, right here?"

I stroked the line of a vein along the right side of her neck from her jaw to where it disappeared beneath her collar bone. She shivered a little, but I was so caught up in remembering that one little detail and how lovingly I'd rendered it on paper that I scarcely noticed.

"Did you know they say that an artist falls in love with every model? It's not that they want to have sex with every model—I'm sure not interested in old man Johnson's johnson—but drawing creates such an intimate connection that you see things that no lover would notice." Lissa took a deep breath and sighed.

"I'm going to have a completely different attitude the next time I model," she said. "So, number two on the list is drawing and painting. What else. What has made you happiest since you've been here at school? What do you look forward to?" I paused for a few minutes and began going down the catalog of my classes. I really did like Art History, even though the class itself was boring. There were moments in Fundamentals and Concepts that I felt excited. Usually when I was mixing paint or had my hands in clay. But those all paled compared to drawing. There was one thing, though, that I really looked forward to two or three times every week.

"Racquetball. It's funny. I just realized that when I'm on the court I get into a zone, just like when I'm painting. Did you know that on court two there's a black scuff on the end wall about two feet off the floor and eight inches from the left corner? It's about three inches long. When I'm centering myself before a serve, I look at that black scuff mark. Everything in the room has a relationship with that one small point. When I hit the ball, I know how far and in what direction from the mark it will hit. I see an opponent's shot come off the wall in relation to where that mark is. I can feel the speed and direction of the ball and know where I need to be to get to it."

"Fuck. You have *got* to teach me that."

"Me? Teach you?"

"I don't think there are more than a hundred racquetball players in the country who would understand anything you just said," Lissa said. "Probably only a dozen who can do it. If it can be taught, I want to learn it. So number three on your list is racquetball. Anything else?" I thought for another minute, but I couldn't think of another thing I look forward to each week. I shook my head.

"Okay, then. Here's the hard part. What do you hate?" That was going to be the hard part?

"Everything!"

"Wrong. You just listed three things that you love."

"But two of them don't have anything to do with college."

"Sure they do. They might not be curriculum, but they are as much a part of college life as Art History. Now, what specifically do you hate?"

"I'm depressed all the time. I hate myself. I hate my life. I hate school. Everybody there is talented and knows what she's doing. I'm a big fraud."

"Tony, look at me." She pulled my chin so I had to face her and get lost in the blue depths again. I wondered if she knew there were black flecks in her irises—all tiny streaks that point toward the center of her pupil. "Tony!" She snapped into focus and I pulled away from the draw of the zone. "Depression is a real, physical malady. It has causes and symptoms. And it can be cured."

NINE

ONCE I STARTED, it didn't take me long to list my top three reasons to hate college. I hated the boring classes where I had to sit without thinking for hours. I hated having so much pointless homework. And I surprised myself when I finally said, "I'm lonely. I have a lover. Two. But I don't have any friends."

When we were done, the water was tepid and Lissa stood and offered me her hand as we got out of the Jacuzzi. I watched the water drip off her body and was drawn to the course it took off the ends of her hard nipples and the flow between her breasts that ran straight down her stomach and into her bare slit. When she reached to hand me a towel she noticed that I'd started to get hard. She grinned.

She gave my cock a little tweak and said, "We need some dinner and you need to get started on your homework." We toweled off and Lissa put on a robe while I pulled my sweats on.

I sat on a stool at the breakfast bar and opened my computer to start writing. Lissa started moving around the kitchen and I thought how motherly she seemed at the moment. I could imagine her making dinner while her two boys sat at the counter coloring. I realized how truly sweet a woman she was.

"Where are your kids?" I asked.

"Jack and I have shared custody. He's offered to keep them more of the time while I'm training."

"You still get along well with your ex?"

"We're good friends. He's a great father to the boys. He realized before I did that I jumped into marriage and a family before I was ready. He's been very supportive. I had savings from modeling and I ended up with this house clear and free. It's a little easier raising children when there are two parents involved. Now work on your paper. I'm not going to talk while I'm making dinner."

DINNER WAS GREAT. She cooked pork chops with braised red cabbage and fennel. Until my few dates with Melody and time at Lissa's house the past couple of weeks, I'd eaten about every meal since September in the college cafeteria. This was absolutely nothing like it. She served me half a glass of cold chardonnay to have with the meal, but told me I couldn't have any more until I'd finished my presentation.

That was another surprise. Aside from glancing up to see Lissa's graceful form beneath the robe moving about the kitchen, I felt less distracted from getting my work done than anywhere at school. I knew most of the material, though I had to look up which grades of cotton duck were no longer in use before I figured out why there were only nine instead of thirteen. Lissa had given me the password for her WiFi and it was actually faster than what I had at school.

Each student was assigned an artists' material. We would give a presentation with a handout for the class. Doc Henredon says we each learn something well and share our knowledge with the rest of the class. I figure it keeps him from having to print handouts himself. And to think that for this class I paid a $100 materials fee.

I finished about eight o'clock. I gave the presentation to Lissa and she just said, "I had no idea!" Then she started to hand me another glass of wine. She held it just out of reach. "Any other assignments due tomorrow or Friday?" When I shook my head she handed me the glass. We sat companionably on the sofa for a few minutes. I glanced over at her and noticed she had allowed her robe to come loose. She wasn't technically exposing much, but the fact that I could see the curve of her breast through the gap and a long bit of thigh below the belt caused a stirring in my groin. Damn, she was beautiful. I reached toward her.

She let me put my arm around her and leaned against me.

"Do I have your attention now?" she asked. "Can we talk without an explosion?" I was suitably chagrined. I knew that I had to make this right with Lissa.

"I'm sorry for acting like an ass this afternoon, Lissa. I really fucked things up, didn't I? I hope that at least you'll forgive me even if they withdraw my scholarship offer."

"Well, they *might* have withdrawn the offer if they hadn't been forewarned about the possibility."

"Who warned them?"

"Who do you think went to the college and asked to authorize you to play?"

"My god, Lissa! Did you...? Oh god, I'm sorry. I just was so... No. I won't go there. There's no excuse. I'm such an idiot. I'm so sorry. Shit!"

"That's a good start. Now come here and I'll show you the next step." She pulled my head toward her and softly kissed me. When she started, her lips were barely touching mine and we just brushed back and forth. As we kissed, she allowed a little more pressure, but her lips, though soft, did not part. It didn't grow into a passionate kiss, but I felt more love in that minute that our lips were together than I could ever remember feeling from just a kiss. She pulled back and smiled at me. She turned her head and released the pressure on the back of my neck while continuing to pet my hair and leaned against me.

"You listed three things you hate about your college experience and three things you love. Most people would say that's a good balance if it weren't for the items on the list. The things you love are all reasonable. Who wouldn't love sex? Painting is the thing that is nearest and dearest to you. And one of the best defenses against depression is exercise. In fact, it's why I took up racquetball."

"What?"

"After my divorce three years ago, I was a depressed single mom with nowhere to turn. My therapist suggested I take up jogging. One week and I said, 'fuck this.' I wanted to beat something. Tennis is too slow. I chose racquetball. In three years I was a national champion. But I can't tell you how many hours I spent on that court. A lot more than you do now," she said.

"Wow! I had no idea. You seem so… together."

"I'm better. But sex, painting, and racquetball aren't enough to combat boredom, stress, and loneliness. We have to see what we can do about that. First, you say the classes are boring. Well, that might be out of our reach for this semester. We can't go around replacing all your classes and instructors. From my experience, having one class you love out of five isn't a bad ratio. I remember one semester where I couldn't stand a single one of my classes."

"What did you do?"

"I withdrew before the first ten days of the quarter deadline, pled a family emergency, and reenrolled in the fall."

"I can't do that."

"Yeah. I didn't have any scholarships and wasn't on a professional program like yours. Let's table that one and move to number two. Too much pointless homework equals lots of stress. How much time do you spend on the class you just worked on? It took you about two hours to do that project and you don't have anything else due this week."

"Yeah, but I'm on call for that stupid mural project all weekend and I have an Art History paper due on Monday, plus midterms. I won't have a chance to work on it or study till Sunday night."

"Except you could work on it tonight and tomorrow night."

"I suppose. But that means... I... we... ummmm."

"Don't worry, sweetheart. After I finish playing mother hen and counselor for a while, I've got a game of lover in mind. Just be patient. There are some things I want as much as you do." She emphasized her point by returning to our kiss. We just savored each other's lips for about five minutes. My wee little pecker was beginning to stretch his muscle... or whatever it's called. "This can be very relaxing, you know?"

"Yeah. I want to make love to you, but I feel like I don't want to move. I could just spend the night holding you like this."

"Do you have a Daytimer?" Well, enough of that little fantasy.

"I keep my schedule on my cell phone."

"How often do you look at it?"

"Whenever I need to write something down."

She laughed. It wasn't just a little snort, it was an all out belly laugh. I didn't think it was that funny.

"Did you hear that? You only look at your reminders when you set them up. You don't look at them to remind you. What good are they?"

"There's an alarm that goes off when something is due."

"Then it's too late to do it. You need to be working on these projects days in advance, not when the alarm says it's due."

"Like not waiting till Sunday night to do my Art History paper. I should know this. I'm in college. I had to do it all the way through high school. There's just no one to…" I stopped and realized what I was saying. I'd come from a close family that held education as the number one priority—before dates, before parties, before racquetball. My dad is a teacher and Mom is just a mom. Not like that isn't enough. Anytime I headed out the door, either Mom or Dad asked if I had my schoolwork done for the week. Not for tomorrow. For the week. I was still waiting for Mom to remind me to do my homework. What a helpless baby I was!

"I'm not going to remind you to do your homework," Lissa said as if reading my mind. "I have two little boys of my own to ride herd on. I don't need a third. But I will help you put together a system where you can see, at a glance, what work you have for the next week or two and then look at it several times a day. Tony, get it off your phone and onto paper. I know that sounds like I'm a Luddite, but you are a visual thinker. If you don't see it in front of you, you don't think about it."

"You're right. It just seems like one more task to do."

"Do it and the others will seem less daunting." She waited for me to respond and finally I nodded.

"Now, the third problem. Tony, don't you have any friends?"

"Um… not really. We see each other in class. We talk in the lunchroom. But until Melody and I came here for that weekend, we'd only spoken to each other at lunch on Fridays. Everybody is so swamped with their classes they don't have time to hang out."

"Ever stop to think that they might have the same problem? Everybody needs friends. You sometimes have to start things yourself, though."

"It's hard. I don't like to talk about what's going on inside me. I have to see those people every day. I don't want them looking at me and thinking, 'There's the kid who misses his mommy', or something."

"Do you miss your mommy?"

"Well, sure. I don't mope around for her, but of course I miss her. And Dad. I miss my best friend Beth who lived a couple houses down from me. And Miss Stone, my high school art teacher. Geez, we'd sit in her classroom after school sometimes and talk about art for an hour. And…"

"Tony. You're homesick." I hung my head. "It's okay. How wonderful that you have family and friends that you miss. You thought you'd replace them all here, and you haven't. In fact, you can't. But there are people here who want to be friends."

"Like?"

"Me." She looked at me and pulled me in for another kiss. This one got quite a lot hotter. When we broke for air, my hand was inside her robe stroking her incredible breast. "Friends with benefits." If a smile can be loving and naughty at the same time, Lissa's came close.

I'D NEVER BEEN alone with Lissa—I mean to make love. In our threesome, she had acted as either the tutor or as the object of our assault. The softness of her kisses was a direct indicator of how she liked to make love. I was half expecting that she'd go wild with just the two of us, but she wanted to go slow and loved soft feathery touches. In spite of the fact that we were both pretty much naked, we made out like high schoolers for an hour before we really got serious. Every step was taken slowly and savored. I think I spent ten minutes just tracing that vein in her neck that caused the extra shadow I'd seen while sketching her. I did it first with my fingers, then with my lips, and finally with my tongue.

I knew for a fact how tough Lissa was. She had muscles where I *wished* I had muscles. But she loved being treated as if she was fragile and I touched her with the delicacy I would use when handling a blown glass butterfly. And she treated me the same way. It was a new experience. I discovered nerve connections between my shoulders and my eyes, my butt and my feet. Little touches in one place would cause my sensors to fire off in a completely different part of my body.

I'm sure Lissa was instructing me on how to make love to her, but she did it without ever saying a word. She touched me and I felt the sensation and then I repeated the touch on her and she moaned. When we coupled, we were facing each other on our sides in almost the exact same position we'd been in while pleasuring Melody over the weekend. Our heads were on the same pillow as we kissed.

I felt my cock—I'd been hard for an hour or more—sliding against her mound. She shifted slightly and instead of being over her stomach I was between her legs. We moved together and her juices joined mine, making her labia and my cock more and more slippery. She reached between us and guided me into her folds. I sank slowly inside and was totally consumed by her beauty.

The position isn't designed for maximum penetration. It's difficult to get very deep but I discovered it provides a lot of stimulation to the clitoris. Lissa glided down the length of my cock with her button rubbing down and back up.

I was shaking and saw that even that was mirrored in my lover. Every stroke caused a new vibration through our entire bodies.

I was so in awe of Lissa that I didn't think of my own satisfaction at all. How could I *not* be satisfied? I just wanted her to be pleased. I wanted so desperately to feel her clamp down on me as she came. And like the feathery touches of our foreplay, we drew this out until neither of us could bear the tension. We clutched each other tightly and our mouths came together in a melding of tongues and lips. I felt her moan more than heard it and my own growl vibrated through her teeth and jaws. Neither of us could deny that we were coming, but the orgasm wasn't centered between our legs. It came from so deep inside both of us that I thought it would rip my lungs and heart out of my chest. I was buried in my friend, my mentor, my coach, my model. But as much as I was in her, she was in me—wrapped in my arms, held in my mouth, and firmly embedded in my heart.

We woke in the morning in the exact same position, and while a little more hurried, the blending of our spirits was just as profound. I barely made it to Fundamentals class on time.

TEN

"**WHERE THE FUCK** were you?"

Man, that came out of the blue. I left Fundamentals class and caught up with Melody to tell her the good news about my scholarship and racquetball, and before I could get a word out she explodes at me. She really doesn't swear that much, so her language took me by surprise.

"What do you mean?"

"I waited in the study lounge till midnight! We were going to work on our Fundies presentations together. You never showed up and then you waltz in here this morning and give a Broadway production while my stupid paper looks like a dog ate my homework and then threw it up. Where were you?"

"Shit! I completely forgot we were going to meet up. I'm sorry. I had so much going on yesterday I was a total wreck. Melody, please forgive me."

"Where were you?" It finally dawned on me that there was only one question on her mind. I cringed a little.

"I was with Lissa. I spent the night over at her house."

"You what? You blew me off to go sleep with *her*?"

"Melody, it's not like that. At least not all like that. I was really messed up yesterday and Lissa helped me get through it. I had to talk it all out with someone."

"And then have sex. Is she your girlfriend or me?" Did I have a girlfriend? I know I told Lissa that one of my favorite things at school was my girlfriend, but she quickly—and correctly—interpreted that as sex. I'd never really considered the implications of actually having a *girlfriend*. Yeah, I'd dated some, but I never thought about it in those terms before.

"Lissa is my... our... friend. She's also my coach. If you'd just let me explain." Melody held up her palm in front of my face. I cringed for a second thinking she was going to slap me. Then she pulled some inner city jive thing on me out of the blue.

"Talk to the hand, asshole. I'm not listening." Then she stormed off and I didn't see her again the rest of the day.

Shit! Just when I thought I might have a handle on my life. I hate this fucking school. Why do I have all this drama? I'm an artist, not an actor, Jim.

————◁◆▷————

I WENT BACK to my dorm room and cut Art Orientation. I stripped, crawled in bed, and pulled the covers over my head, determined not to come out until they closed the dorms for the summer.

Of course, I didn't silence my cell phone and it started chiming once every ten minutes with messages until I finally gave in and got up to see who was texting me. I hoped it was Melody. I really didn't mean to hurt her and it never even occurred to me that my being with Lissa would upset her. We were both with her all weekend. Is that what it was like to have a girlfriend—always wondering if you were going to upset her over something stupid? I scanned through the messages but her name didn't pop up. There were messages from both Sandra and Amy, from John Gilbert at the gym, wanting to set up time with me this afternoon, and from Dean Peterson asking me to stop and see him after my painting class on Friday. I was about to open Sandra's message when a new message came in from Lissa. I looked and it said simply, "Have you picked up a Daytimer yet?"

That really brought me up short. I'd blown off the athletic director and trainer at the club yesterday and that reflected badly on Lissa. She'd gone to bat for me to help with my depression and I owed it to her not to embarrass her again. It was 2:30. Technically I should still be in class, but I'd already missed two thirds of it, so I decided to head first to Staples and then to the gym. I texted John and asked if he could meet at 4:00. I was on my way downstairs with my bag slung over my shoulder when the message chimed again and his response was simply, "Yes. CU then."

While I was walking I texted Lissa and told her I was on my way to Staples now. She sent back a smiley face. I finally popped Amy's message open. "WTF?" was all it said. Jolly. Not only was I in shit with Melody, but with Amy and Sandra, too. The three musketeers. By then, I was at Staples, so I didn't bother to open Sandra's message.

I spent half an hour picking out a planner. I had no idea how many different kinds of these books they had. I didn't know anybody still used paper calendars. Everybody I knew kept their schedules on their cell phones. But I loved what I was seeing. Let's face it. I do think visually. I kept thinking of what Lissa said about me needing something that was big enough to see ahead and not just what was due now. There were daily and hourly journals, journals that had places for expenses, travel arrangements, and receipts, auto journals, weekly journals, monthly journals. They even had bigger planners that you could post on your wall and use erasable markers on. That was kind of cool, but I thought I needed something I could carry with me if I was going to make it work.

I finally settled on a teacher's planner. It had a column for each of the five days of the school week and a sixth column split between Saturday and Sunday. The days weren't divided with rigid times, but were just "Morning, Afternoon, Evening." It was also nice because it was an anytime calendar. You wrote the dates in at the top of the page so I didn't feel like I was paying for a year and only getting nine months. For good measure, I bought a really nice mechanical pencil that had a large enough and soft enough lead that in a pinch I could use it to sketch with if I couldn't think of anything else to put in my planner.

I was definitely ready. I headed for the gym.

———◁◆▷———

THE ALARM ON my phone went off at 4:00 p.m. and I was standing outside John Gilbert's office. It wasn't really *his* office. All the trainers kind of shared one big room with desks in it, but as far as I could tell they used whatever desk was free when they had a break from training. John led me into the office and several other trainers glanced up at me curiously. We sat on opposite sides of an empty desk and John got out his schedule.

"Coach wants us to work three times a week. Two times in specified strength training exercises, mostly with weights or the machines, and once in Pilates. I watched you play and you've got incredible reach and flexibility, but you won't believe how much Pilates will extend you. You've got two hours of court time scheduled on Monday, Wednesday, and Friday, so we get Tuesday, Thursday, and Saturday unless you'd prefer Sunday."

"Two hours of court time? I usually only play for an hour."

"Lissa extended the court time to two hours, but she might be intending half of it to be her training."

"Is she doing weights and Pilates, too?"

"Yeah. She always does. I can get you in at the same time if you can be here at 6:00 in the morning."

"She trains at 6:00 a.m.?"

"And she's a wild woman in the morning. She works out before she has coffee and you do *not* want to cross her."

"I'm not even human until after lunch. Do you have any afternoon slots?"

"I do. What's your schedule?" I laid out my new planner and pencil, then pulled out my cell phone.

"I've got classes from nine till noon and one-thirty to three-thirty on Tuesday and Thursday."

"I see. So you're free from noon till one?" He grinned at me. Right. Like I was even going to get here and back in an hour. "How about setting things up at four? Can you get here that fast from class?"

"It's not far, but I don't get to eat much on those days. I just grab a sandwich in the cafeteria to choke down between classes."

"It's okay to grab a sandwich or some fruit and yoghurt before you work out, as long as it's not too heavy. You shouldn't work out on empty, though. We need to figure a way for you to get nutrition during the day. I'll talk to your coach about it. For now, let's set up 4:00 for training Tuesday and Thursday."

"Is this going to be two hours, too?" I was scribbling in my new planner, transferring my class schedule for the next week into the planner.

"No. The workout will only be an hour, but you'll probably want to cool down and then hit the showers before you leave, so allow time for that. Can you be here Saturday morning at nine?"

"I'm on call for this stupid mural project from noon until midnight on Saturday and noon until nine Sunday this weekend. Next weekend spring break starts."

"We've got a great Pilates trainer who can take you at nine for forty-five minutes if you can make it."

"I'll do it."

"You're a lot more cooperative today than you were yesterday." I looked at John. Time to mend a bridge or whatever the expression is.

"I was kind of an asshole yesterday, John. I hope you'll pardon me and that we can work together."

"What kind was that?" He looked at me and grinned. He leaned across the desk toward me. "You know, I've only been out of college for three years. I thought I was going to get a teaching job as a high school coach. I ended up here as a personal trainer. Shit happens. I'd have been just as pissed off as you were. I'm glad you got through it so fast."

"Thanks. Do we have time for a workout today?"

"I'd like to show you the routine. Here." He reached below the desk and pulled out a white polo shirt and blue warmups. "We've been informed that you are now a member of our team. You're welcome to wear the blue and white."

I got changed and then joined John in the weight room. The machine he put me on was a mass of cables and weights on a glider. He handed me what looked like a handle on a rope and showed me some twisting exercises that caused the weights to rise when I pulled on the rope. It wasn't a lot of weight, but ten reps on each side and I was done with that. Little did I know that after ten reps on each of six different machines, he would run me through all of them again. In fact, I did three sets before he told me to stretch out and cool down.

Weight training works your muscles differently than actually playing. I could tell that I was going to be sore tomorrow. In the locker room, I took a long sauna and soaked in the hot tub before showering. All the time I was in the tub, I kept thinking of Lissa naked beside me. All we were doing at the time was talking like any two guys in the locker room, chugging down water. What magic switch did she flip that turned her from a fellow athlete relaxing her muscles into an irresistible sex object? She was so far beyond me I couldn't even imagine understanding her.

ELEVEN

I **WAS GOING** to stop for fast food at a burger joint, but thinking about the fact that I was in training, I went into the local Larry's Market to get a salad and some cooked meat from the deli instead. Lissa told me I needed to keep up my protein intake and cut out some of the fats. I wondered if I would ever be able to eat in the cafeteria again.

It was after eight o'clock when I stumbled into my dorm and headed to my room. I was exhausted.

I was not prepared to find Sandra sitting in the hall with her back against my door. She started to speak to me when I walked up but I held up my hand.

"Please don't ask me where the hell I've been," I said with as much emphasis as my current state of exhaustion would permit.

"I just wanted to check in on you, Tony. I could tell when you disappeared after class that Melody hit you pretty hard. She's the sweetest girl in the world and a great friend, but she can be a bitch if she doesn't get her way."

"Thanks for checking, Sandra. I'm doing okay. I'm sure we'll talk tomorrow." I opened my door and stepped through and Sandra came into the room right behind me. I've got a roommate, but I haven't seen him all this term. I think he has a girlfriend he stays with all the time. There's a half full cup of soup on his desk that's been there for three weeks.

"Ooo, gross." Sandra obviously noticed the cup. I shrugged.

"My roommate is a pig. I don't know; I haven't seen him in so long he could be bacon." She laughed. It was a nice sound. We missed our Friday lunch last week because of the long model sessions that Lissa did for Figure Painting. I mean, you miss one and it's two weeks between meetings. Maybe that's what Lissa was talking about when I complained I didn't have friends. I didn't know where my roommate was. Sandra was standing here and just because I didn't have lunch with her last Friday, I missed her. I hadn't said two words to Amy since lunch week before last. And aside from Melody, these were the people I shared the most classes with. I should probably spend some time just catching up. I pulled out my desk chair and slid it over to her and plopped back on my bed.

"Tell me about your week, Sandra. It's seems like forever since we've talked."

"What? Are you reading that out of my text to you?"

"Huh?"

"I texted you three times today. Didn't you get them?"

"Oh damn. I got so many text messages today I didn't get through them all. I was kind of busy." I pulled out my cell phone and saw that instead of the one message I saw before I took off, there were two more from Sandra that came in while I was working out. 'Are you okay? I'm here for you,' was the first one. 'Seems like a long time since we caught up. Doing anything tonight?' 'I'm just going to sit by your door till you get there, so please don't stay out all night. We need to talk.'

"We really need to talk?"

"What? You think I'm just using it as an excuse to get in your stinky dorm room?"

"I could use a Coke. Want one?" Sandra nodded and I got two Cokes out of my mini-fridge. I should have been drinking water just to rehydrate, but if Sandra wanted to talk, I was going to need caffeine and sugar. I surprised myself when I blurted out, "How's Melody doing?"

"She's pissed. She hung around all afternoon hoping you'd show up and then was hurt that you disappeared again. Amy's with her."

"Why aren't you with her?"

"There are only two of us and two of our friends are hurting. I won the coin toss."

"Friends?" I only hung out with Sandra and Amy at lunch on Fridays. Of course we were in a couple of the same classes and groups of us would get together to study or be in the studio at the same time working on our projects, but we didn't interact all that much. I rolled over on my side and looked at Sandra sitting on my desk chair.

She was cute. There was no real sexual attraction between us other than the obvious male/female teenager kind of thing. If we were the last two people left on earth, I was pretty sure we'd try to procreate. Probably if we were in the last million or so. She was barely over five feet tall—even shorter than Melody, though plumper. Like most of my classmates, her clothes were black. Hell, so were mine. How pretentious could artists be? There isn't a mark on the scale for that. I was seriously considering starting to wear Hawaiian shirts and board shorts just to express my individuality. They'd drum me out of the Artist Corps.

Sandra was a little on the round side. Zaftig would be a good word, and no, Margaret Cho, it doesn't mean fat pig. Her hair was kind of strawberry blonde and she had the complementary green eyes to go with it. Sometimes you didn't notice them because she used a lot of eyeliner that took attention away from her eyes.

I guess I'd just never thought about her as really a friend. She was more like an accessory for Melody. But here she was, sitting in my room saying she won the toss and got to talk to me. I smiled a little and just repeated the word. "Friends."

"I didn't come here to talk about Melody," Sandra went on. "How are you doing, Tony?"

"Better now than earlier, but still pretty miserable. I really didn't mean to hurt Melody. I was so overwhelmed yesterday that I couldn't think straight and Lissa was there to talk to..."

"Wait! You were sleeping with Lissa? The model? Oh my god!"

"Uh... I thought you knew. Melody didn't tell you?"

"All she would say was 'I trusted her' and 'I thought she was my friend.' She'd never say exactly who she was talking about. Lissa?"

"Lissa is a really good friend of mine. Of ours. She's really more than a friend."

"Obviously! Geez, no wonder Melody is so upset."

"Huh?"

"Tony, you idiot! What girl could compete with that goddess? Melody probably feels like you don't think she's good enough or pretty enough."

"That's ridiculous. Lissa has been nothing but supportive of Melody and me. She plays racquetball with me. She's teaching Melody. She modeled for us. She taught us... stuff. She..."

"Slept with you."

"Yeah, but it's not like she hasn't slept with Melody, too."

"What? Oh my god!"

"Oh shit. I shouldn't have said that. Sandra, you've got to forget I said that. I'm going to kill myself."

"Before you or after you slept with her?"

"Well, we… um."

"Oh my god, together? And then you went to her alone? She's not only brokenhearted, she's jealous!"

"Of Lissa?"

"Of you."

"Why would Melody be jealous of me?" This was way too confusing for my pea-brain to figure out. In fact, I couldn't figure out how Sandra was getting this. It was like she was some super-conduit for reading Melody's emotions. "Wait! You mean Melody wanted Lissa?"

"Duh!"

"That can't be right. I've got to go talk to Melody."

"She won't see you right now. She's pouring her heart out to Amy. Why do you think I'm here?" Sandra got up and set her Coke can on my desk then came to stand right over me. "I'm here to be your friend." She began stroking my forehead. It really felt nice. It was so soothing and comforting. I got to thinking about how Mom would touch my forehead when I was sick as a kid. I was sick.

I was sick in the head. I couldn't turn my mind off and I kept getting more and more depressed. But Sandra was telling me everything was all right. My eyes drifted closed. Her fingers massaged my scalp and ran down the back of my neck. "I'm here to comfort you." I wasn't sure that was what she said, but her hands had moved to massaging my shoulders and then down to my pecs.

There was a little hesitation in her moves, but then she resumed her massage, moving down to my ribs and abs. I'd had a pretty tough workout with the weight machine this afternoon and everything she was doing felt really great. I felt a light brush across my lips. Her hands were both working on my abs, so I thought for a moment that she gave me a lovely little sisterly kiss. She brushed my lips again and when I softened to kiss her back a little, something slid into my mouth.

My eyes shot open. This was no sisterly kiss. Sandra's head was thrown back so far I could hardly see her face. Her breasts were bare and her left nipple was pushed into my mouth.

I spluttered and struggled to sit up.

"Don't worry. It's okay. It's just a little friendship. I'm with you and Amy's with Melody." I shook my head and tried to comprehend what she'd just said. Somehow a girl having her tit stuck in my mouth didn't seem like a friendship thing.

"You mean Amy is having sex with Melody?"

"I should hope so. We figured you'd both get relaxed enough to finally talk if we took a little of the edge off."

It was really hard to concentrate on what that meant with this lush mound shoved in my face. Then Sandra's hand found my already erect prick. *Oh shit!* Hadn't Melody alluded to this kind of thing a while back saying she thought about inviting Sandra and Amy to join us before we found Lissa?

But I don't trust them exactly.

I sat bolt upright on my bed and pushed Sandra away from me. Her breasts jiggled as she sat down in the desk chair. God, her areolae were huge. They covered half the front of her breast with hard nipples the size of my little finger. She sat staring at me without bothering to cover herself. She was grinning at me and repositioning herself slightly every few seconds to call attention back to her breasts.

"I'm sorry, Sandra. You'd better get dressed and leave now. I'm not going to start my relationship with Melody by cheating on her."

"But you already had Lissa."

"Lissa is different. Melody knows that and I think now so do you." She began to pull the straps of her shirt back up, but before she covered her breasts she spoke again.

"Are you sure? A little oral satisfaction might help you relax. I could just nurse you to sleep."

"Sandra, please." She looked a little disappointed, but she finished dressing and put her jacket on. She picked up her books and turned to me.

"You really are special, Tony. I'm jealous of Melody, but I won't ever interfere again. I thought maybe it was just a little infatuation you two were going through, but I see it's serious. I don't know how your relationship with Lissa is going to work out, but I'm jealous of you, too. 'Bye." She left and I breathed a sigh of relief. She's a sweet girl, and she's got a lot of curves in the right places, but I had other girls on my mind.

I grabbed my cell phone and had Melody's number tapped in before I stopped and stared at the phone. Melody clearly wasn't ready to talk to me, and even though I thought Sandra was making things up, I didn't want to risk hearing Amy with her when I called.

I switched to messaging and tapped out, "Miss you. Gnight love," and hit send.

I WORKED ON my Art History paper and actually got most of it finished before I finally crashed and went to sleep. Sometime in the middle of the night I felt my phone vibrate. I was going to ignore it, but something made me look. It was a text from Melody. It just said, "U2."

———————◁◆▷———————

AMY GRABBED ME after painting class Friday and dragged me down to lunch. When I had my food, she escorted me to a table where both Sandra and Melody were seated. Melody started to get up and leave, but Sandra dragged her back down in her seat.

"Sit and be quiet. Both of you," Sandra said. She can be pushy at times. I'd seen evidence of that last night. "Amy and I have something to say to you and you both need to hear it at the same time. Then you can go on being mad or not talking or stupid or whatever if you want to. First of all, I went to see Tony last night." Melody snapped around toward her, but Sandra kept going. "He got home about eight o'clock and I was sitting on the floor next to his door. He hadn't answered a single one of my texts all day. We went into his room and I tried to seduce him."

"You bitch!" Melody blurted out. She started to get up again, but Sandra hadn't let go of her yet.

"I am. But let me finish. I tried *unsuccessfully* to seduce him. I even took my top off and tried to get him to suck my nipples." I couldn't look up, but it didn't take a direct look to see that Melody had her mouth wide open. "What Tony said to me, I will remember for as long as I live, and I will be forever jealous of you, Melody. He said, 'I'm not going to start my relationship with Melody by cheating on her.' I just thought you should know that, and I'm sorry I made the play and I won't do it again."

Man, that took guts. I had a new admiration for Sandra. She didn't let it sit around as some little secret that she could use later. She came right out and said exactly what happened.

"Is that what happened, Tony?" Amy asked. I nodded. "Well then, it's time for me to speak. Last night I met Melody for dinner. I took her to a nice restaurant and talked for hours about Tony and what had happened. I knew Melody was bi from conversations we'd had before, so when we got back to the dorm, I kissed her. Sorry you haven't had that experience yet, Tony, but when I kiss, I kiss good. I tried—I really tried hard—to seduce her."

"And I said Lissa was the only woman in my life," Melody broke in. Amy looked at Melody and I could see the color rising in my girlfriend's face. Was she really telling me that Lissa was who she wanted to be with?

"Not good enough, Mel," Amy said. "She said Lissa was the only woman in her life *and* that she would never mess around behind Tony's back."

"Is that right, Melody?" Sandra asked. Melody's blush was almost crimson and she was looking at the table. She nodded without raising her head. This had gone on quite long enough. I reached across the table and lifted her chin with my finger. She finally brought her eyes to mine.

"Melody, I don't know where all of this is going, but I know that I want to find out with you. I think I love you." She faltered for a second and then a shy smile crossed her face.

"I think I love you, too, Tony."

"I've got so much to tell you."

"Let's talk on the way to the gym."

"Awww." Sandra and Amy said together. "They're so cute."

"Tony?" I was surprised by the voice behind me. I turned and almost dropped my lunch tray.

"Dean Peterson! I'm sorry. I missed our meeting after class. I was kind of waylaid. I didn't even look at my calendar after class."

"You'll have to get better at that. A calendar isn't worth much if you don't look at it."

"Yes, sir."

"Let me get a sandwich and we'll walk back to my office." He turned away from me and I sank back in my chair with a groan.

"What's going on, Tony?"

"I was supposed to meet with the Dean after class and you dragged me here instead. Not that I object to the results, but I have to go see him again, now."

"Again?"

"I had a meeting with him after Art History on Wednesday."

"Is that what everything was about?"

"Yeah. Look, I've got to go. I'll see you at the club, Melody. Sandra, Amy, thanks."

TWELVE

"I**T'S ALWAYS GOOD** to get feedback from your peers. What did your friends think of your new status?" In spite of me blowing off our meeting, Dean Peterson didn't seem upset with me. He was casually eating his sandwich and drinking an iced tea while we talked.

"I haven't told anyone."

"Does that mean you still aren't sure that you want to take this opportunity?"

"No sir. I do want to take advantage of this and I want to thank you for considering me. I just haven't had a chance to talk to anyone except my coach since we spoke. I had a lot of… well, I didn't respond too well when I met Mr. Jacobson and John Gilbert at the club. I was feeling pressured and sort of blew up at them. I haven't been able to talk to Mr. Jacobson since to apologize, but I did start training with John. I'm hoping the school will still consider me for this program."

"Tony, that was well said. You *do* need to apologize to Sam, though I think he understood what was going on. I warned him that it was too soon to approach you, but he was so enthused that he wanted to go right over and watch you practice. Nothing has changed regarding the offer, but I needed to hear from you that you accept."

"I accept, sir. I won't let you down."

"Tony, have you been to student counseling services?" I looked at Dean Peterson.

"I'm not crazy, Dean. I just got a little upset is all. Lissa helped me see what was going on."

"Then you are aware that over half of the incoming freshman population suffers from the same things that you have been? Loneliness, depression, feelings of inadequacy, stress, isolation."

"How do you know I felt all that?" I suspected Lissa had talked to him and it pissed me off a little. She had no right to discuss what I told her in confidence.

"Like I said, over half… I could list symptoms one after another and even plot on a calendar within a week when students would feel them. I'm not minimizing it or suggesting that your problems are typical. It affects each student differently, some more than others. I'm only suggesting that there are people here who would listen to you and understand. They might even help. It's up to you, of course."

"Thank you, sir. I'll make an appointment."

"Don't forget to write it in your calendar and then look at it." He smiled at me. "By the way, you mentioned Lissa. I wasn't sure, but I assume you mean Coach Grant."

"Yes sir. I've known her for quite a while before she was my coach. Is it improper to refer to her by her first name now?"

"Possibly when you are at a competition. People should know your relationship is a coaching one." He breathed a sigh, shook his head a little, and then went on. "Tony, I don't mean to pry, but do you have more of a relationship with Miss Grant than just friends and fellow athletes?" I swallowed hard. I didn't want to get Lissa in trouble, but I had a hard time just lying to the Dean about it.

"Sir?"

"Okay. I'll withdraw the question. Relationships between faculty and students are frowned upon and faculty members risk their jobs if they become involved with a student. I get pretty protective of students in that regard. And it is my student that I am concerned about here. However, Coach Grant is not a faculty member. The college does not pay her. Nor does SCU. She's a volunteer and a well known member of the athletic community. Since she is still quite a young woman, I will not pretend to monitor your relationship. But be careful, Tony. It's not unusual for athletes to worship their coaches. Just track how many Olympic athletes are married to their coaches. Make sure you are making choices based on what you want and not on what a beautiful woman can convince you to do. Do you understand me?"

"Yes, sir. Thank you, sir."

"You are still very formal with me. I used to play a little racquetball myself, you know. I wouldn't mind coming down to the club to volley with you some time if you don't mind. I'll wait until after the Intercollegiate, though."

"Thank you, sir. I'd be happy to play you some day."

———◄◆►———

"TONY, TAKE MELODY onto the court and work with her on her backhand for a while. I want to see the ball in motion, but you two need to talk. Don't get wild. Now go." Lissa summarily sent us into the racquetball court and plopped down outside to start stretching.

I served to Melody's backhand and she swung wildly.

"It's the same as a forehand swing," I said. "Just not quite as powerful. When you bring the racquet back, concentrate on keeping it perpendicular to the floor. The tendency is to let it drift down at an angle. Then when you swing you don't have as much surface area ready to meet the ball. Try it again." I served again and the next time she made contact. I lobbed two more to her. Her returns were becoming more dependable.

"Why did you go to Lissa without me?" The question came just before I served and I couldn't answer until she'd returned it and the echo died.

"I was really upset. I blew up at some people who were really important and Lissa calmed me down. We went to her house to cool down and talk." Serve. Return.

"Couldn't you talk to me?"

"Lissa was a part of what I was upset about. I couldn't even *see* straight when she took me out of the club." Serve. Return.

"The stuff with the Dean? Are you in trouble, Tony?"

"Not exactly. But it was so overwhelming I didn't know what to do." Serve. Return.

I stopped and turned toward Melody before she could ask her next question and just shook my head. She waited.

"I wanted to tell you Thursday morning when I saw you. Then I realized how badly I messed things up. So I haven't told anyone. I was waiting for you. The school has given me an opportunity to earn a double degree in a new program with SCU," I said. "And they want me to play in the National Intercollegiate Racquetball Championships next month. I know I should have been shouting and screaming and rushing to tell you, but all I could see on Wednesday was more stress and pressure. I've hated college ever since I got here. Lissa talked me down after I blew up at SCU's athletic director and helped me see that it wasn't really about college. Until you and I got together, I felt so alone I couldn't stand it. And then Lissa was a part of what we had and I never thought about being with her as separate from being with you. I wasn't trying to cut you out and I didn't think of it as cheating because I can't think of life without both of you. I'm still so confused I can hardly breathe when I talk about it. Melody, I love you and I love Lissa. Does that make me some kind of freak?"

"It makes us both freaks because I love you and I love Lissa, too. I just thought you'd *chosen* her instead of me, and that she'd chosen you instead of me. I'm sorry."

Serve. Return.

"Tony, are you going to play in the Championships?"

"Yeah."

"And you've agreed to do the double degree?"

"Yeah. That's what Dean wanted to talk to me about this noon."

"How are you going to afford it all? How will you ever get the work done?"

"I'm scared to death, Mel. I'm scared I'll fail everyone. They offered me a full ride scholarship and Lissa helped me start to get organized. But, Melody, I know I can't do it if you aren't with me, too." Her racquet fell to the floor just before I served and the ball went whizzing past her as she launched herself at me. Before I knew what was happening, Melody's lips were plastered against mine and her legs were wrapped around my waist. I kissed her like she was the first drop of water from a mountain stream. I drank her in. I held her and stroked hair and her back. It was heaven and I only barely heard the door close behind us. Melody and I turned our heads together to see Lissa leaning against the back wall.

She looked relieved and sad at the same time. She was looking at us with a half-smile and her lower lip caught between her teeth and I thought I saw the glint of a tear in her eye. It was the first time I think I ever saw her look uncertain. I looked at Melody and she put her feet on the ground. She nodded and we both rushed Lissa and swept her into a hug and covered her face with kisses. In seconds, we were all giggling and kissing each other. When we finally stopped for air, I looked at the two women I'd fallen madly in love with. We had to find a way to make sure each of us knew what our relationship was. I had an inspiration. I took Melody's hand and pulled her so we were facing Lissa.

"Lissa. I… we were wondering. Would you go steady with us?" I thought she'd split her sides laughing. She looked at us and hugged us both.

"Yes, I'd love to go steady with you both. I can't believe it, but I think I'm in love with both of you." I thought Lissa had been the instigator of all this at one time, but then I thought we'd done pretty well at declaring what we wanted. There was still something missing, though. Melody seemed to pick up on it right away. She pulled away and took hold of Lissa's hand and the two looked at me.

"Tony, Lissa and I were wondering if you'd like to go steady with us. We really, really like you." I felt this silly grin spread across my face and it almost locked my jaw too tight to answer.

"Yes," I croaked out. "I'd love to go steady with the two of you. I love you both." We all collapsed in on each other with more kisses and hugs, then Lissa took the lead and grabbed me by the hand. We stood facing Melody and Lissa spoke.

"Melody, Tony and I really like you and we were hoping that you'd maybe like to go steady with us." Mel was giggling so hard now that she had trouble getting the words out. Tears were running down her cheeks. I couldn't tell if it was just because she was happy or because she was laughing so hard.

"Tony and Lissa, I love you both and I would love to go steady with you!"

———◁◆▷———

IT WAS ALMOST two hours later that we got to Lissa's house and were all immersed in the spa. We each had a liter bottle of water and Lissa was insisting that we had to drink all of it before we could leave the spa and play. We were doing a pretty good job of playing in the spa, though. Someone was kissing someone or groping someone or lying on someone all the time. I soon discovered that I got as much pleasure out of seeing Lissa and Melody kissing or hugging each other as I got out of kissing either one of them.

And there was something else. I had a feeling that it took a while to identify. Of course I felt sexy and loved. I felt happy. But under all that I felt something else and I finally decided that it was hope. All the time I'd been depressed this year, I'd felt so hopeless—like I'd just set foot on a path that I could never change and I would be miserable for the rest of my life. Now I felt hope that things would be better, that I wouldn't be lonely, and I wouldn't be a failure in everything. I drank a little more water and savored the feeling. I was so spaced out, just thinking about it that I almost inhaled a lungful of water when the two girls swept in on me and dunked me.

———◁◆▷———

AFTER DINNER, WE made love. We weren't frantic or so hot and horny that we couldn't wait for each other. We were passionate, but we were exploring how to be a three-person couple. Does that make sense? We had to figure out who got what body part. And the disagreements weren't all about who got the one cock among the three of us. I smashed noses with Melody when we both dove into Lissa's pussy from opposite directions. We discovered that our laughing sent a new kind of vibration through Lissa and she came as Melody kissed me with our cheeks resting on her labia.

That didn't stop us from turning our heads and both sticking our tongues into her as far as we could reach. *Oh god!* To feel Melody's tongue sliding against mine while we both licked at Lissa's clit was so incredible that I came. Melody felt me splashing against her stomach and it set her off and when she screamed into Lissa's pussy, Lissa came again.

Best of all, though was the three of us cuddled together with our arms around each other as we went to sleep about midnight. I lay awake a few minutes after their breathing had settled into the even cadence of sleep and tears ran down my cheeks. My life *wasn't* going to hell.

Or at least if it was, it was going in a luxury limo instead of a handbasket!

THIRTEEN

MY **ALARM CLOCK** on Saturday morning consisted of two incredibly beautiful women smothering me—and each other—with kisses. I think that when we fell asleep last night, I was more or less between—or maybe under—both of them. I woke up early once and Lissa was sprawled next to me on her back with my arm under her neck and her right leg thrown over my left. Melody was laying half on Lissa's left leg with her head pillowed on Lissa's left breast. I reached across and put my hand on Melody and went back to sleep.

At seven, I woke up to both of them giggling and kissing me. I was pretty aroused—what guy isn't when he wakes up in the morning—but they wouldn't do more than give me a little squeeze now and then. We hit the shower together and playfully scrubbed each other clean. This time when we stepped out of the shower, I was given the job of drying both of them with a big towel while they made the task difficult by continuing to kiss and grind themselves against each other.

We finally dressed and had breakfast. Lissa said she'd take me to the club for my morning Pilates class and then I was on my own.

"I looked at your Daytimer," Melody said. "Did you?"

"Not yet. I know what my first appointment is this morning."

"And what comes next?"

"More beautiful lovers in my arms?"

"Tony." Lissa handed me my schedule. I flipped it open and saw the weekend assignment. I was on call to work with my Fundies prof on the mural from noon till midnight today and noon till nine on Sunday. I'd completely forgotten.

"Oh yeah," I said. "Shall I meet you after I'm off?"

"No," Lissa said. "Go back to your dorm and sleep in on Sunday. Then do your second shift and get enough sleep Sunday night to get to your class on time Monday. I'll see you on the court Monday afternoon. See? It says so right here in your calendar."

"What are you guys going to do?"

"We 'guys' are staying right here for some girl time."

"Lissa said she'd pose while I do some painting."

"All day?" I asked.

"Of course not, silly. Only when we're not having sex!" I'm sure my chin must have hit my knees when my mouth fell open. I could feel my cock bounce up in my shorts and threaten to escape. Lissa and Melody were going to spend the day together painting and making love while I was slinging plaster for my prof's stupid mural. How could they? The image of the two of them in my mind, though, was so erotic that anger was short circuited and my cock was rigid. Before I was aware of it, I felt two hands on my cock and two sets of lips on my neck. Then they joined me in a tender three-way kiss.

"That will give you something to think about while you're getting all hot and sweaty with Dr. Henredon," Melody said.

I smiled. Actually, the image of the two of them *would* be a pleasant thought while I was working. And I was going to be way too tired to do anything when I was done.

Mural

"As my folks used to say back in Nebraska," I drawled, "what's good for the goose is good for the gander. I hope you two have fun."

I meant it.

———◁◆▷———

PILATES LOOKS LIKE a calm and peaceful activity. There are machines that help you move your body, devices like a huge ball that you lie on, no real weights clanging around or anything. The focus for me was core strength and flexibility. I had no idea how exhausting a workout it could be. When I was done, I hit the sauna and shower, got dressed, and went to get a big burger on the way to the project site. I justified it on the grounds that it would probably be my last meal this weekend.

I arrived a few minutes before Doc Henredon, who was pleased to see me already there when he pulled up in his van and had me help unload his equipment and supplies. We walked into the administration building where one hall had been blocked off and scaffolding was set up. It wasn't monumental, like a Roman cathedral or anything, but it was still a big wall about forty feet long and fifteen feet high. The mural had been commissioned by the school to show the arts in action. I'd looked at the sketch and rendering. It was like one of those big sports murals by LeRoy Neiman only, instead of Olympic athletes, it had scenes of dancers, theater performances, sculpture, and all that. Pretty much everything that was taught in the college would be represented in the mural. It wouldn't cover the whole height of the wall, but would cover the whole length. A four-foot-high wainscoted panel guarded against scuffs in the high traffic area. Dr. Henredon said the hall wasn't wide enough to let people stand back and view something that went so high, so the actual painting would be about eight feet high by forty feet long and meant to be seen in pieces.

I was involved a few weeks ago on the weekend we fastened fiberglass mesh to the wall. After that, a fresh coat of plaster was applied and Dr. Henredon supervised every step of making sure it created a perfectly smooth and even surface. I had to hand it to him. He didn't just hire a bunch of contractors to come in and plaster a wall. He was a stickler about every detail and students who worked on his project learned to do work that hasn't been common since the Renaissance.

One of our most interesting classes near the end of last term was the debate on whether it should be done as a *fresco*, a *buon fresco*, or a *secco*. The difference is in how wet the plaster is and the type of paint you use. Doing a *secco* on dry plaster was a compromise between trying to teach a classic technique and working with the practicalities of being a part time project with student help. In a lesser school than PCAD, they might have just painted out the wall with Kilz and then started painting the mural with interior latex. Doc felt his students would learn more if it was done in a classical manner. I guess he was right since I was standing there thinking about the different techniques while he gave me a tour of the sketch and the pencil drawing on the wall.

I started to grouse about the fact that none of the other student assistants were here yet and it was already a quarter till one when Doc stopped me.

"They will not be here until two."

"I thought call was at noon."

"I have one student with me for a couple of hours before the others arrive so we can get to know each other a little better."

I had to admit that I was enjoying the individual attention. He'd explained to me what issues of perspective had to be considered when painting on a wall and that you had to think about where the normal viewer would be standing. The hall was too narrow to get back far enough to view the whole painting at once. Most people who viewed this massive work would be four to twelve feet away. I had always assumed that a muralist would either lay in all the background and then work forward, or he would start at one corner and work outward from there. I could see, however, that there were scattered pieces painted or sketched along the wall. So I asked about the order things were being painted in.

"Focal points. The wall was primed and then covered with gesso. We blocked out the wall in a grid pattern that matches the grid on the rendering at a 1"=1' scale and then roughed in the drawing on the wall. Now we are painting the focal points. These are the points that people will be drawn to as they walk down the halls. It is where I focus my attention. As they are laid in, I ask students to paint in the negative space."

"But the rendering shows a lot more figures. Are you planning to paint them over the background?"

"Yes, exactly. The paints are technically opaque, but as you know, that depends on the consistency. If we cut the pigment with clear varnish, the background will show through. As a result, we can use the exact same hues for the background images and the tone will be reduced, pulling those images into the background and away from the focal points."

"Wow!" It was really a neat concept and I hadn't heard of other artists doing that, though I wasn't all that familiar with murals outside of our class. "Will I be working on negative space today?" Even though it would be essentially flat, painting negative space was something you could see the results of in a short period of time.

"No, Tony. I have a special job for you." Dr. Henredon led me to one of the five focal points that were still unpainted. It was a studio setting of a nude lying on a daybed and reminded me of something. "I believe you are familiar with this model. I'd like you to do the focal painting." He handed me the rendering that he'd been carrying as he talked to me. It was Lissa. And I'd swear it was rendered from one of my sketches. Only this was at least three times larger than I intended to paint her. It was slightly bigger than life.

"That's my... the model from our class and my sketch."

"I always look through Professor McIntyre's final project sketches to see if one merits inclusion in a larger project. Do you think you are up to rendering it at this size?"

That was a problem. The only reason I hadn't recognized the sketch on the wall in the first place is that it looks a lot different at that size. I got off the scaffolding and took the rendering to the opposite side of the hall. I looked from the rendering up to the sketch on the wall and at last I could see it. The question was could I paint it?

"Bravo. You did the one thing most first-time muralists forget to do. You stepped back to where the viewer will be."

"Do you think I can do this?"

"You are showing talent, Tony, and I have you for another nineteen hours. I think you should try."

"But what if I mess up? If you don't like it…"

"Then I'll paint over it and render it myself. But I don't think I'll need to, do you?"

"No sir."

"When you paint a mural of this scale, you begin by laying in the general tone, but only work a portion at a time. Follow the edge where there is sharpest contrast, put in the base color, and add the shadows while it is still wet. I know you have used acrylics before, so you should be able to mix these colors and control them fairly well. The tricky thing is that you have to mix a lot more paint than you would for a canvas. At the same time, with the gesso coating, you will not have as much paint absorption as you would on canvas. The plaster is pretty well sealed."

"Yes sir. Does every student in Fundamentals paint a segment of the mural?"

"No. Some never deal with paint at all. Some sketch. Some sling plaster. Some will varnish the wall. But this year, you are the one invited to work on a focal point."

———◁◆▷———

BY THE TIME I was ready to start, the other two helpers for the day had arrived. Robert Bragg was a spaced out guy I knew only from the Fundamentals class. I think he was studying computer graphics, but he always smelled like pot. Kate was a cute girl—the fifth freshman in our Figure Painting class—who was just plain stuckup. I don't think she'd spoken two words to anyone since school started. She was a good painter, though, and when she saw me working on the sketch when she got there she got a weird expression on her face like I was a bug that should be squashed.

I did some erasures on the wall sketch and revised it some. It took a while because I kept getting off the scaffold and crossing the hall to look at what I was drawing. Part of the reason I hadn't recognized Lissa was because it had been transferred to the wall so poorly. I had to work on remembering what it really looked like. This was different than portrait painting, even though I *was* painting a portrait. It was more than life size and I was going to use a smooth acrylic paint rather than oils.

Acrylic has some real advantages. It's easier to clean up with soap and water, mixes quickly, and is a nice consistency for brush work. It also dries faster than oil. That's great for getting a canvas finished and off the easel quickly, but it can make wet blending a bitch. After I'd spent a good two hours revising the sketch I realized I didn't have any of my own brushes with me for applying the paint. I went to Dr. Henredon to ask if I could go get my brushes.

He was working on the figure of a dancer at a different focal point. I got lost in watching him for a while. I must have stood there for half an hour before Robert made a wisecrack about me loafing while they were working. Doc didn't turn or say anything. There isn't a lot of conversation when a group is working on a project like this. Doc was in a zone. It was an unspoken rule that when an artist is in a zone like that, you simply don't disturb him. I watched what he was doing and identified the red sable brushes he was using as he deftly brought the figure to life.

I could see what he meant by following the chiaroscuro or the curve of tone contrasts that ultimately define the depth of the work. On a canvas, you have a lot of flexibility in where you work, usually starting with the general background and working forward. But I could see that on a wall where part of a face could be as big as a normal canvas, you needed to look for drying points that were easy to blend and define.

I tore my eyes away from what he was doing and walked down the hall to where Kate and Robert were working together on the negative space. They were talking quietly together and I could see that they were doing a lot more than just slinging a background color in between focal points. The background was gently textured and they were doing a careful job, referring frequently to the rendering.

"You need the rendering?" Robert asked.

"No that's okay. Nice job on that texture. Have you watched him at all?"

"No," Kate said. "He told us to come down here, showed us what to do and told us not to bother you. What gives?"

Her greeting was none too friendly and this was more words than I'd heard her speak all year. Figure Painting is usually a sophomore or higher class and the five freshmen in it all had to present portfolios to the professor in order to be admitted. Needless to say, Kate was good.

She had black hair that she wore in a ponytail to keep it out of her way. Both she and Robert were wearing white painter's caps. She wore bib overalls over a sleeveless t-shirt and you could see where she'd wiped paint on her pants over the course of several projects. She was pretty tall and nicely proportioned. She was working barefoot and I noticed her toes were neatly manicured and the nails painted a brilliant purple. Everybody has their thing, I guess.

"You should model," I said without thinking.

"Yeah. I hear you're into 'You show me yours and I'll show you mine.' But I've already seen you and I'm not about to return the favor."

"What?" Robert broke in. "Tony, you exposed yourself?"

"Naw. They convinced me to step in for a missing model for one of our Figure Drawing classes last semester. I wore a jock."

"That's okay," Kate said. "I saw all I needed to. And his girlfriend's seen more from what I hear."

"Uh… look. Daniel Smith closes in half an hour and I need to run out and get a couple of brushes. If Doc comes out of his zone and looks for me, would you tell him where I went?"

"Sure. Is that our class model, Lissa, you're working on?"

"Yeah. I'm scared shitless about actually starting to put the paint on the wall."

Kate looked at me strangely.

"I'm sure you'll do great at that like everything else you do. We'll tell him if he asks." There was a hint of jealousy in her voice. She went back to her work and it felt like I'd been dismissed and maybe even snubbed.

FOURTEEN

I DON'T KNOW if they intentionally situated an art school near an art supply store or if the store saw a ready market and opened nearby. I know the store has been there a long time and I was a frequent customer. Most of my student loan probably found its way into their cash register. I justified it by saying it was all an investment in my future career, so I didn't buy cheap stuff. I'd watched Doc Henredon painting for long enough to identify the kinds of brushes he used and I walked out of the store with one hog bristle and three sable brushes and about $120 poorer. I ran by the dorm and picked up my art box and sketchbook as well. I didn't buy brushes that I already had.

It was nearly six o'clock when I got back to the hall and before I'd set up to start painting, I heard the soft chime of Doc's cell phone alarm.

"Let's take a break," he said after a couple of minutes spent finishing a stroke. About two minutes later a pizza delivery guy showed up with three boxes and a carton of Cokes. We all dug in and Doc asked to see the brushes I'd brought back. He nodded his approval and gave me a couple of tips about how to use each one. He wasn't at all upset that I hadn't started putting paint on the wall yet and walked over to look at the adjustments I'd made on the sketch.

"This is good. Is she really that beautiful?" I was surprised by the question.

"Yes, sir. I mean you saw her when you did the rendering, right? She's incredible."

"No. If I'd seen her, I'd have fallen in love. I used one of your sketches that Professor McIntyre gave me to put in the pose."

I was a little startled. I thought he'd stepped into the studio while I was sketching and did a sketch as well. I would never have known.

"Kate, I need the scale drawing," Doc called. I was closer, but Kate came from one end of the hall to the other to walk past us and pick up the drawing about ten feet away. She had a scowl on her face as Doc turned before she got back and walked back to where I'd been working. I heard a bit of a huffy sigh behind me as Kate followed along. Robert was totally absorbed in a phone conversation down the hall, but when he saw the three of us walking toward him he hung up and came to meet us. Doc took the sketch from Kate.

"My god! Look what you did to this sketch!" Doc yelled. All three of us jumped back from him. I started to apologize but he waved me to silence. "Look! All three of you. Here is the drawing I did based on Tony's original sketch. It's a generation removed from the original. Look at what he has drawn on the wall. This is what 'an artist falling in love with his model' means."

"Tony?" Kate looked at me strangely.

"Yes, yes," Doc said. "I did not draw from the model. I drew from his sketch. My drawing is technically correct but lifeless. Tony has drawn this model and I would guess has even painted her." I nodded. "Look at the eyes. It is not only how the artist sees the model; it is how she sees him."

All three of us just stood there staring. I think Doc was giving me a compliment. Kate was sneaking sidelong glances over at me and then up at the sketch on the wall. I'm not sure Robert had tuned into the fact that Doc was speaking. It wouldn't surprise me to find out he was high.

"Tony, don't paint her tonight. It's no good to start right after you've been praised or criticized. I hate doing it myself. Someone comes up and talks about all the wonderful things I've done and I can't paint a single decent stroke afterward. Spend a couple of hours doing drapery. Learn how your brushes feel and the texture of the paint. Come back tomorrow morning and start fresh on your lover." This was really freaky. Could he possibly know that Lissa was one of my two very precious girl-friends? Or was he just talking about the metaphysical connection between artist and model.

"Um… call said noon tomorrow."

"If you prefer. It is Sunday. This is my sanctuary. I will be here at 8:00. Come when you wish."

Robert wandered back down the hall to where he was doing texture painting. Kate stood there looking at the scaled sketch and the drawing on the mural for a minute, then took the sketch back to Doc's easel. As she walked by me on her way to do more background, she turned to look at me. She made one of those gestures that people do to look threatening, but for her it looked more like a hint of expectation. She pointed two fingers at her eyes and then pointed them at me. It's the old, 'I'm watching you' gesture.

TWO HOURS LATER, I'd laid in most of the surrounding drapery and worked various highlights and shadows in to make them look almost like deep blue velvet. It took a while to get used to the new brushes and to accomplish wet blending the way I wanted it. I wasn't really satisfied with it. I always loved painting drapery, whether it was hanging from a window or just folds in people's clothes. In a way, I even thought of skin as being draped on the skeleton and muscles, so it was a kind of drapery, too. But these looked isolated and mechanical. One fold of fabric was completely disconnected from the next. It just didn't look right to me. I was getting frustrated.

"You started earlier than the others today," Doc said. I jumped at his voice behind me. It was about 10:30. "You should get some sleep. You can redo this tomorrow."

Redo it. He could see that it sucked, too. What was I going to do? I knew while I was painting that he'd be judging the quality of my finished work, and I was acutely aware that Kate kept glancing at me. I knew what was missing, but I just wasn't able to get into the zone like I had while I was sketching.

"Doc, would you mind if I brought a headset with me tomorrow? I like to block out distractions with music."

"Eh?" He pulled an earplug out of one ear and showed it to me. Smiling he said, "Do what you need to do."

I gathered up my things, cleaned my brushes and palette, and headed back to my dorm. What I needed to do was sleep in the arms of Lissa and Melody. But I wasn't about to interrupt their girlfriend time. I'd selfishly had Lissa to myself without a thought about Melody on Wednesday and the two of them deserved time together. I did send them a "goodnight-love you" text message.

I LAY IN my bed—alone—and kept thinking about the painting. I could see Lissa in that position. I knew every contour and every shadow. But every time I saw the painting in my mind's eye, it was wrong. I grabbed my sketchbook and started leafing through all the pictures. I even looked at the painting of Melody that I'd completed when I thought I was working ahead for class. Just looking at her eyes and the way she was smiling at me was almost too much to bear. She was so beautiful I thought my heart would break.

I looked at the many sketches I did of Lissa. Some of them were from class during the marathon drawing session on Friday. Some were from that weekend at her house. Some were of the poses that she did for Melody and some for me. Then I found one that always made me smile. It was the first drawing of her at her house, just after Melody and I made love to Lissa the first time. She was lying back on the daybed with the drapes gathered around her and that perfectly sated smile on her lips. Melody had all but passed out, kneeling on the floor beside her with her head and arm draped across Lissa's stomach. I'd just stood up and when I saw them I whispered, "Wait. Don't move." I'd done a hurried sketch, but it was my favorite among them all.

I didn't hand that one in. For my formal sketch—the one Doc used for the mural—all I did was move Melody out of the picture. Lissa was in the same position. I thought maybe I'd have to do another pose for my final project in figure painting now that this one was being done in the mural.

I nodded off to sleep with the image of Lissa and Melody on my mind and dreamt of my two lovers together.

FIFTEEN

I **WOKE UP** before dawn. I mean, I really woke up. I felt like I wouldn't need sleep again for a year. I was so jazzed I grabbed my stuff and was out the door within five minutes of waking up. Just before I left, I stopped and grabbed the sketchbook with my original sketches in it. I stopped at the all-night Starbuck's a block from campus and the only person in it was a sleepy-looking barista who did her best to smile at me when I came in. I got a shot in the dark—a dark roast coffee with a shot of espresso—and a bagel sandwich and headed back out the door. I noticed the barista had pulled two shots and dumped them both in. I'd leave a bigger tip next time I was in.

There's a big church a few blocks away from campus and in the half light of dawn I made my way there. I don't know what kind of church it is, but it's big and has lots of stained glass windows. Maybe it's Catholic or Lutheran. The Baptist churches back home didn't have stained glass. The doors were unlocked, but I didn't see anybody around when I went in. I found a seat in the middle of the sanctuary and looked up at a wall of stained glass behind the pulpit. It was about three stories high and had a religious scene portrayed in it. The transfiguration, I think, but it didn't really make a difference.

What I cared about was that it was a clear day out and it was nearly sunrise. I could already see color beginning to spread through the nave. I put my headset on and started my music playing. The subtly muted strains of Orff's *Carmina Burana* started, hauntingly distant, but growing closer. By the first timpani, the sun had broken the horizon and the entire nave was a riot of color. Energy from the music was being pumped into me. The espresso wasn't hurting either. I swallowed the last of my bagel and drank off the remaining coffee. I stood in the center aisle and waited. In just a few moments the light from that big stained glass window touched me.

> *Hac in hora sine mora*
> *corde pulsum tangite;*
> *quod per sortem sternit fortem,*
> *mecum omnes plangite!*

I turned and ran out the doors of the church with my bag and tossed the garbage into a receptacle near the sidewalk. By the time I reached the hall and *my* painting, my heart was pumping a mile a minute. I didn't even stop to greet Doc. I just started pulling together the paints that I was going to need. Half a dozen buckets of acrylic paint were open on the scaffolding and a dozen small jars of pigment were nearby when I started mixing the colors I wanted on my palette.

Her forehead is impossibly high and so smooth it looks like polished stone. It's covered by locks of fine golden hair that sweep across from a boyish part in a hairstyle that reminds me of Peter Pan. I remember the first time I kissed her right at the place where that part begins and found the skin that looked so opalescent was soft and warm. It was incredible. I stayed there with my lips gently touching that spot for what seemed like hours while I held her to me. Debussy's *Prelude to the*

Afternoon of a Faun was playing as I mimicked the texture of her skin with the softness of my brush strokes.

I couldn't see her left ear in this position, hidden behind her aristocratic cheekbone. The right ear was slightly different than the left. There was an extra fold of skin leading to her inner ear. I'd played with that fold with my tongue teasing her until she scrunched her shoulder up, almost touching the ear, and I couldn't get to it any longer. Then I lay my head on her shoulder and lightly blew up into her ear. The ferocity of the kiss she turned and planted on me made me forget everything else in the world. There was nothing but her lips touching mine.

Those lips might seem a little pale compared to the garish colors girls around school wear for lipstick. I'm sure she was wearing a little makeup when she posed for the class, but when Melody and I did our sketches in her basement she put no makeup on at all. You could almost see the nerve endings lying so close to the surface that a single touch of the lips caused her to tremble. Her lips were parted, not in a toothy grin, but sensuously soft as if to welcome a lover's kiss. I remember placing my lips there and tilting my head slightly to the left as our noses grazed against each other. I lived that kiss again and again.

Her nose couldn't be straighter or more perfect if a Greek sculptor had cut it out of stone. When she was aroused, you could see her nostrils flare slightly. I closed my eyes once and traced the length of her nose up to the slight impress between her eyes, then let my fingers trail across her almost nonexistent eyebrows. It was her eyebrows that convinced me she was naturally blonde. The pale gold wisps were only visible if soft light caught them and cast a shadow against her brow. Nose and brows together brought all the focus on her face to her incredible eyes.

Her eyes. I saw immediately what I'd unconsciously been trying to do with the drapes. I was picking up her eye color in the velvet drapery. But I'd been missing my light source. I could always get lost in Lissa's eyes. She has incredible intensity. The black streaks in her pupils deepen what would otherwise be a pale blue. When I look into her eyes, I see into myself. She shows me what I could be. Sibelius's *The Swan of Tuonela* was playing as I lost myself in those eyes again. The fleck of golden candle light reflected in her eye as she looked at me—loved me.

Lissa's shoulders were elegant and powerful at the same time. I'd watched her in matches with other players at the club and you can't put that much English on a ball unless you have both power and control. To see her muscles move in her shoulders and upper arms is like watching a dance with an entire ensemble supporting the prima ballerina. But to see those muscles up close...

While we made love I lay on my back and she supported herself on her arms. The drive of her hot, wet pussy was not a hip thrust movement. Her entire body undulated and I saw from only inches away how her shoulders, biceps and pecs worked together as she used her arms to force her way back onto my cock. When she drew forward until only the glans was in her, her breasts raked across my chest like hot coals. Those muscles shifted beneath her skin, drawing it taut across her collar bone and pulling the concave between her neck and shoulder even deeper. I caressed the joint with my lips and felt her push back against me again.

Beethoven's *Symphony #3, Eroica* found my face between the lush, perfect mounds of her breasts. I haven't been up close to that many breasts. I have looked at a lot of pictures—for research. One thing that I've noticed is that a woman's breasts are almost never identical. A nipple or areola is a slightly different size, or just off center. One breast is firmer than the other and doesn't flatten as much when she lies down. But that is not how it is with Lissa. You could hold a mirror perpendicular to her sternum and not have a more perfect match in the reflection than in her other breast. When, in my naiveté, I asked her if she'd had implants she started laughing.

"You have no boundaries, do you?" she howled. Then she explained that when she was modeling she was almost completely flat chested, but that during pregnancy her breasts had filled out and never shrank. Gravity had simply had much less time to work on her than on other women her age who matured earlier. But when I touched them with my fingers, or the tip of my tongue, I thought of them as being holy. They were too perfect for anyone but a goddess.

All I could think about was how Melody and I had advanced on Lissa standing in front of the sleigh bed that was my setting where we first made love. Together we worshipped all of Lissa. We kissed together; we petted Lissa's arms and back; we suckled at her breasts. Melody guided my cock when I entered her as she lay back on the bed. Melody peppered Lissa's stomach and mine with little kisses, working her way up first to my lips and then to Lissa's. We made love to her as one person, always seeming to know what the other's hand or mouth was about to do, as if it were simply an extension of our own.

I erased the rest of the sketch and didn't bother to redraw. Tchaikovsky's *Symphony #6, Pathétique* washed over me.

Melody had been the first ray of hope to enter my depression. What I thought was a hopeless fantasy turned into a mystic reality when she asked me to model for her. Melody had brought us to Lissa's house that first weekend and not only did we paint, we gave each other our virginity. Each time I looked into her lavender eyes I was struck with the impossibility of us being together. Yet, even when I'd done something stupid and been wrapped up in my own misery, Melody was there. I embraced her softness and felt her respond to my touch.

Her skin was slightly darker than Lissa's almost translucent beauty. There was a fine spray of freckles across her shoulders. Her auburn hair spread out in a fan across her neck and Lissa's abdomen where she lay in sated exhaustion. We had not only pleasured Lissa, we had reached a new peak with each other and our orgasms were as intense as Lissa's. Lissa's left hand hung down off the cushion behind her, just touching Melody's hair. One finger was raised slightly toward me. Melody's arm lay across Lissa just above her Delta of Venus, casting those delicate curves into deep shadow. Melody's thighs and the lower part of her beautiful butt were also cast in deep shadows, being below the level of my light source. I'd stroked those beautiful cheeks with my hand and my face until Melody had drifted to sleep pillowed on Lissa's stomach. You could see the fingers of her left hand entwined with the fingers of the other woman's right hand, held tightly at the edge of the bed.

Away from the light source, the figures quickly fell into darkness. The flame on the single candle drifted slightly to the right as though a passing ghost had pulled the fire with it. It seemed to take only a few strokes to correct the shadow and depth of the drapes I'd painted yesterday. I could hear the strains of Enigma's *Cross of Changes* playing in my ears as I made last loving adjustments to a shadows and highlights.

I stood in front of what I had painted. Two of the most incredible women I'd ever known. My friends and my lovers, clasped together as I knew they had been all weekend. It filled me with such overwhelming joy that I stood there with tears running down my cheeks as I listened to the last refrain.

> *You'll see the face who'll say,*
> *I love you, I'll kill you.*
> *But I'll love you forever.*

As it faded, I emerged from my zone. I felt a little dizzy and my mouth was dry. I pulled the headset out of my ears as I dropped my brush on the scaffold. I heard a whispered, "Holy fucking Christ!"

When I turned toward the voice, I saw a crowd of people. My entire figure painting class was there with Professor McIntyre. Doc Henredon was standing watching as was Dean Peterson and most of the students from Fundamentals and Figure Painting. Melody and Lissa were in front and they both had tears running down their cheeks. I had no idea when they'd arrived or how long I'd been painting. I know I took a break a little after noon to use the restroom and get a drink, but I hadn't taken my headset off and I went right back to the scaffold without even looking at anyone else.

Doc Henredon started it. Then everyone was clapping. I must have looked like a deer caught in the headlights and I knew I was still crying, but right in the front of the crowd were Lissa and Melody and they were crying, too. Then someone shouted, "Sign it!" and soon everyone was chanting "Sign. Sign. Sign." I looked at Doc and he nodded to me. I looked at my brushes and palette lying on the scaffold and selected a half-inch round sable brush with a twelve-inch handle. I dipped the brush into the deepest blue I'd applied to my drapes and in the space just before the painting faded into complete shadow, I signed my name. When it was dry, it would scarcely be noticeable. I didn't want my signature to detract from the painting.

When I finished, there was another cheer and I got down off the scaffold. Melody and Lissa rushed me and I was squashed in a hug. We each kissed the others, completely oblivious to what was going on around me. I was so exhausted and thirsty, though, that I finally croaked out, "Water. Restroom." The crowd parted as I rushed into the men's room and pissed like there was no tomorrow. Geez! What time was it, anyway? When I came out, Lissa handed me a bottle of water and I gulped it greedily.

Doc Henredon, Professor McIntyre, and Dean Peterson were all standing about six feet in front of the painting with students all around them.

"It's the light," Doc was saying. "A single candle flame. Look how the figures float in the darkness that surrounds them, lost in their own world. But her eyes show an awareness of what is passing beyond. She is a tigress that has just feasted, but can't help noticing the gazelle that is grazing nearby. Look at these muscles—relaxed, but ready to leap in an instant. The finger becons to her prey. And my god! The second figure. Kate, tell them what you saw." Kate was standing nearby and was surprised at Doc's request. She picked up the narrative, though.

"Um… He was working down the figure and as he blended the colors, she seemed to fade out, like he couldn't move the brush farther down. Then he grabbed an artgum eraser and erased the rest of the sketch. He started putting the second figure in without even sketching her. It was like he'd memorized it and just kept painting. And look at how beautiful she is!" Kate was shaking her head. Doc picked up the narrative.

"Even though you can't see her face, her position is so peaceful and at rest that you can see the love between the two women. She doesn't grip her frantically. She is not a supplicant. She lies peacefully, content as the smile on her lover's lips."

"Who is it?" someone asked. Everyone turned to look for me. Lissa and Melody had shifted away so they weren't near to me. I looked at Professor McIntyre and she smiled.

"Um… a friend. A very good friend," I said.

"He worked nonstop for like eight hours this afternoon," Robert spoke up.

"And nearly five hours before that," Doc said. "Tony, I was afraid to interrupt you and tell you to take a break. You were so deep it was as if you were in a trance. I'd like to listen to your soundtrack sometime." I smiled and nodded. All I wanted to do was collapse.

"People, it's after nine. You should all get home and get some rest before classes tomorrow."

I HAD TO clean up my brushes and palette after everybody filed by congratulating me. They all had to stop and put their shoes on before they left. There was a big sign inside the door that said, "Shoes off! Absolute silence!" It was closer to 10:00 by the time I was ready to go. Kate surprised me by staying behind to help with cleanup. She kept looking at me and then over at Melody and Lissa as they waited. I was so hungry my gut was trying to digest itself. I'd long since finished the liter of water that Lissa gave me and was hoping we'd find ourselves at Red's

Burgers before long. We all walked out of the building together with Doc Henredon.

"Good work, Tony," Doc said. "I'm proud to have that piece in the mural."

"Thank you Doctor Henredon."

"Uh, Tony?" I glanced over at Kate. She was still looking nervously at Lissa and Melody. Finally, she plowed ahead. "I changed my mind. Anytime you want." Then before I could respond or even figure out what the hell she was talking about, she turned and ran off toward the dorms.

I turned to my lovers, my eyes pleading.

"Take me home?"

Also by Devon Layne
*(Now available as Kindle eBooks.
Print versions coming soon!)*

The Model Student Series
Book One: Mural *(Now in Paperback!)*
Book Two: Rhapsody Suite *(Now in Paperback!)*
Book Three: Diva *(Paperback coming soon)*
Book Four: Triptych *(Paperback coming soon)*
Book Five: Odalisque *(Paperback coming soon)*
Book Six: The Prodigal *(Paperback coming soon)*

Erotic Paranormal Romance Western Adventures
Redtail *(Now in Paperback)*
Blackfeather *(Paperback coming soon)*
Yelloweye *(Coming in 2017)*

Visit DevonLayne.com for more books!